The Executioner's Blade

MISSION POINT PRESS

Readers are encouraged to go to www.MissionPointPress.
com to contact the author or to find information on how to
buy this book in bulk at a discounted rate.

Published by Mission Point Press
2554 Chandler Rd.
Traverse City, MI 49696
(231) 421-9513
www.MissionPointPress.com

ISBN: 978-1-950659-07-4
Library of Congress Control Number
available upon request

Printed in the United States of America

The Executioner's Blade

J. R. Seeger

book 3 in the   MIKE4 series

CONTENTS

AAR: after action report

Alpha: Surveillance terminology for a target location of interest.

Bravo: Surveillance terminology for a person of interest.

BTK: Acronym for below the knee amputation.

Charlie: Surveillance terminology for a vehicle of interest.

COS: Chief of Station. The senior CIA officer in a field station.

CPU: car pickup

CQB: Close quarters battle aka urban assault operations.

CSM: Command Sergeant Major. The senior non-commissioned rank in the US Army.

CWO: Chief Warrant Officer. A military rank with ratings from CWO1 to CWO5

DCOS: Deputy Chief of Station. The number two officer in a CIA station.

Downrange: A generic term applied to any combat tour.

FOB: forward operating base

Foxtrot: Surveillance term for walking surveillance, in contrast to vehicle surveillance.

FWD: forward. When a command is split in multiple locations, each of the locations outside the main headquarters are listed as "fwd." In this story, both Balad airbase and Bagram airbase have a SOF(FWD) contingent.

Glock: An Austrian pistol manufacturer. Glock pistols in this book are Glock19 (a compact pistol) and Glock26 (a subcompact pistol). Both are chambered in 9mm.

Green eyes: Night vision goggles, aka NVG.

Head of station: UK term for the head of the British intelligence in a field station. Also, "station commander."

HF: high frequency radio transmission.

HOA: Horn of Africa

HUMINT: human intelligence

Klingon: Military terminology for intelligence collectors, especially CIA operators in the field (see also OGA).

Makarov: a small, Russian officer's pistol. Similar to the Walther PP in design, it is chambered in a 9mm x 18mm cartridge

M4: US Army military rifle with a collapsible stock and short barrel chambered in 5.56mm.

MP5: A short-barreled submachine gun chambered in 9mm.

NAVSPECWAR: US Navy Special Warfare Command

NVG: Night vision goggles

OP: Observation point

OGA: "Other government agency" — a military term for the CIA.

One up: Surveillance term for working in a vehicle without a partner.

PCS: Permanent change of station — a long term assignment.

QRF: Quick reaction force. A military unit on standby to support a smaller force if necessary.

Red Gun: A non-functioning plastic training weapon with approximately the same weight as the real gun. Originally, all training weapons were colored red. They come in other colors as well, but are still called "red guns."

RTU: "return to unit." If a SOF operator does not meet the necessary requirements, he or she can be returned to their parent unit in the conventional forces.

SAP: "Special access program" — a program which has a limited and classified audience.

SAS: Special Air Service — a UK Special Operations unit.

SBS: Special Boat Service — a UK Special Operations unit.

Selection: A formal training program used by special operations units to select candidates.

Serial: A surveillance term used for a single, continuous shift following a target or observing a location.

SF: US Special Forces, aka Green Berets.

Shooters: Special Operations teams specifically trained to conduct raids.

SIGINT: signals intelligence

Six: The call sign for any commander of any military unit. Therefore, if the overall call sign for a unit is Mike, then Mike6 is the commander of that unit.

SMG: Submachine gun

SOF: Special Operations Forces

Squint: A less than positive name for analysts focused on imagery intelligence.

Standby: A surveillance communication term implying new information.

S&R: Surveillance and Reconnaissance — a fictitious US special operations unit.

SVTC: Secure Video Teleconference

Tag: An electronic tracking device.

TDY: Temporary Duty. A short-term assignment.

TF160: A unit from the US Army Special Operations Aviation Regiment. In this novel, they fly MH60 "Blackhawk" or MH8 "Little Bird" helicopters

TOC: Tactical Operations Center

Two up: Surveillance term for working in a vehicle with a partner.

Victor: Vehicle

VSO: village stability operations, a Special Forces counterinsurgency mission

Zero: The call sign for the team leader on a surveillance team.

ZULU: Greenwich Mean Time. When operations are conducted across multiple theatres, they are all linked to Zulu time so there is no confusion on what time they are starting.

No proposition Euclid wrote,
No formulae the text-book know
Will turn the bullet from your coat,
Or ward the Tulwar's downward blow.

Strike hard who cares –
Shoot straight who can –
The odds are on the cheaper man

"Arithmetic on the Frontier"
Rudyard Kipling

SETTING THE BOARD

T he U.S. Air Force C17, inbound from Iraq, seemed to hover, barely moving above the horizon. Watching from the runway parking apron, Chief Warrant Officer Sue O'Connell of the U.S. Special Operations Force wondered how the huge cargo jet could appear to rest so lightly on the air. She realized it was an optical illusion, but it was still a marvel that anything that big could fly at all. It was 1800hrs and O'Connell stood on the tarmac next to her British Special Boat Service colleague Warrant Officer George Marklin. Sue was wearing her NOMEX flight suit. George was in his UK NATO green camouflage known as disruptive pattern material or DPM. Neither was wearing a beret: Flight line rules said no headgear that could be sucked into jet engines.

George turned to Sue and said, "Before the aircraft lands and we can't hear shit from the jet engines, I need to know, who are these guys and do you know them?"

Sue shifted her weight to her right leg, easing pressure on the prosthetic attached below her left knee. In the years since the firefight had taken her lower leg, Sue had adapted to the nearly unconscious adjustments of position that eased the discomfort without giving away she was a "below the knee" amputee or BTK. She had learned to keep those adjustments invisible to anyone who didn't realize she was a BTK wounded warrior. As to the prosthetic, Sue wasn't certain if George knew about her injury and she wasn't one to bring it up. She'd proven to herself and to the SOF operators who knew her that the injury did not affect her work. She saw no point in raising doubts in anyone else's mind, especially her UK colleague.

Sue smiled, "I know these guys very well. They were my second family for about five years as we hunted terrorists from before the attacks on 9/11 and then into Afghanistan for several years afterwards. They are known as "the MIKEs" because of their callsigns. You and I worked with some of them in Iraq and Syria. Honestly, I miss being MIKE4. Chief Jameson, MIKE6, saved my life." Sue paused to collect her emotions. "What I don't know is why they are here."

George nodded. He and Dozer had worked with the MIKEs with Sue in Syria, tracking down a "dirty bomb" plot as part of Operation MACE. "As to why they are here," he said, I can help, at least a little. The command is having a big gathering tomorrow. Some sort of follow up to MACE. Since that was very "need to know," it may be Command wants to keep the new Op inside the family. More than that, I don't know. All they told me was to be there, all present and correct, at 1400hrs."

"That explains my instructions as well…" Sue's voice was drowned out by the arrival of the C17. It landed in a rise of rain as the wheels hit the ground and the large cargo aircraft did a smooth taxi off the runway and toward the parking apron. The RAF ground guide raised the two orange signal lights in his hands and guided the aircraft toward the parking slot just ahead of Sue and George. Sue and George put on blue ear protectors that doubled as their firing range ear protection. Conversation would have to wait.

As soon as the clamshell doors on the aircaft opened, Sue could see the passengers and crew responding to the difference in temperature and the humidity. At the SOF base in Iraq, it was still warm and always dry. In Cyprus, summer was transitioning quickly into a cool, damp autumn. Even with the smell of aviation fuel, Sue could smell everything that made the island green. Sue watched as the Air Force loadmaster pulled out the wheel ramps and unshackled the vehicles in the aircraft. She heard the vehicles starting up well before she saw the team. They drove off the C17 in two right hand drive vehicles: a Range Rover and a Vauxhall Vectra, and a left hand drive VW minibus. The VW was modified to serve as the radio command vehicle and command center for any and all electronic surveillance equipment that the team might use in the field and was known as "the Magic Bus." In the vehicles were her old teammates from Surveillance and Reconnaissance (S&R) Squadron of the US Special Operations Forces. As the Range Rover drove off the aircraft, Sue saw Chief Warrant Officer 5 Bill Jameson at the wheel. The MIKEs had arrived.

Sue realized she was grinning from ear to ear. It had been a long time since she had been this happy. "Boss, welcome to paradise. What the heck are the MIKEs doing here?" Sue shook hands with Jameson and then worked her way around the team. Each gave her a bear hug.

When she rotated through the team and returned to Jameson, he said, "I wish I knew. One day we are working up in Kurdistan and the next we receive orders to borrow two vehicles from our SRR mates and relocate ASAP to Cyprus. Now, don't get me wrong, we think this is a lot better than Kurdistan…" nods all around from the team, "but we only know that orders came through to help on a project here on the base. You have anything resembling quarters for us?"

Sue wasn't sure how to answer. Since she had arrived in Cyprus as the lone intelligence collector for the SOF human intelligence unit known by its Ft. Bragg address, Warehouse 171, Sue's "quarters" had been a shipping container filled with communications gear, a safe that held her communications and her weapons, a wall locker for her clothes, and her single bunk. "I don't know, but we can ask my Brit colleagues." She turned to George and said, "Any ideas?"

While Sue was on good terms with George's SBS section and George knew Jameson from MACE, she also had observed that the British team was very possessive of their space in the aircraft hanger where they bunked when they were not in Iraq. She expected they would not necessarily welcome a group of newcomers into what they defined as "their RAF hangar."

Jameson broke the ice by offering his large, scarred hand to Marklin. "George, good to see you again. I hope this time we aren't looking at breaking any international laws, but you never know with O'Connell." The SBS team leader took Jameson's hand with a welcoming grin.

"Bill, it is good to see you again. Cyprus is a lovely spot for R&R. The rest of the team should be around sooner or later." As if on cue, two more Land Rover Defenders pulled up with the rest of George's SBS team. They got out and started to introduce themselves and ask the questions that SOF operators always ask: Who are you? (First name was enough.) Where are you coming from? (Since 9/11, it was most often, Iraq or Afghanistan.) And what do you do?

Jameson spoke for the team in sentences short enough to get the introductions out of the way. "We are part of the SOF Surveillance and Reconnaissance Squadron. Basically the American counterparts to UK Special Reconnaissance Regiment. I went through SRR selection in Hereford and advanced training along with several seniors from S&R. We then set up our own selection process. We were just pulled from Iraq. The rest of the team are in the vehicles: that's Billy, George, Deke, Joe, and Nate. Probably the best guy for you is Nate. He is our driver/mechanic and if it has an engine, he can make it run better."

Each of the guys had raised a hand from outside the windows of the vehicles as Jameson ran through the names. The British SBS team did the same as George pointed to the guys who had pulled up, "You know Dozer from Syria, the rest of my pirates are Mac, Paddy and Brian. We came to help off-load your kit, but it looks like you are sorted. If you want to follow us then lets get off this apron before the RAF police give us hell."

Sue was glad to see the introductions were without drama. She had noticed in the past that even among SOF operators, there could be a bit of testosterone competition. No effort this time from either side to prove who was the toughest. She also noticed that Billy was driving the Magic Bus and seemed to have become a fully integrated member of the MIKEs. Back in Afghanistan in what seemed a lifetime ago, she had wondered if he was going to make it. Jameson and his deputy at the time, Jim Massoni, didn't seem certain and neither did Sue.

She said, "Anyhow, we are all supposed to stand by for a visit by the COS tomorrow. She will meet us in the base commander's conference room at 1400hrs. I think the base commander wants you there as well."

Jameson turned to George and said, "Is there any place on base where we can get quarters? We don't need much more than bunks so long as you let us keep our kit and vehicles in the hanger? "

George confirmed the meeting time, adding; "As to bunks, I may be able to find temporary quarters on base housing. After all, you are here at the request of the base commander, so who's going to object?"

"Brilliant."

The base commander's conference room looked like every other military conference room Sue had seen. Beige walls. Brown wooden table. Burgundy government-issued desk chairs for the principals and straight-backed chairs along the walls for the rest of the crew. Doors on opposite sides of the rectangular room allowed access. At one end of the table, the commander's chair. At the other end, a large plasma screen for video teleconferencing.

Sue sat along one of the walls with Bill Jameson and George Marklin. They were ten minutes early which in military time meant they were on time. Slowly the rest of the room filled up with participants in US and UK uniforms. The only participant that Sue recognized was the US military attaché, Col. Jack Williams who had been her local boss since she arrived in Cyprus. At 1400hrs exactly, four principals arrived in the room and sat behind prepositioned name cards: RAF Akrotiri base commander, Air Commodore Neil Bereford; SIS Cyprus Station Commander John Monford; BSS Commander, Jeremy Chartwell; and COS Nicosia, Patty Dentmann. As soon as they sat down, the plasma screen lit up with four separate boxes titled "Vauxhall," "Langley," "Balad" and "COBRA" which George informed Sue was "Cabinet Office, Briefing Room A," the UK venue where issues of national security were discussed. Four faces appeared on the screen. Sue didn't recognize any of them except the SOF operations chief, Colonel Harry Chambers.

"Shit." George spoke under his breath. "That's the SBS commander in the COBRA."

Sue looked over and whispered "Luckily, it doesn't appear we have a speaking role and I don't think the camera has a wide enough lens for him to see you."

The Base Commander opened without any formal introductions or prelude, "We are here today to discuss a counterterrorism threat on Cyprus that has been revealed through a set of joint UK-US operations in Cyprus and Iraq over the past six months. The two programs, SLINGSHOT and MACE have focused specifically on terrorist efforts to build complex weapons designed to attack both our troops in theatre and innocent civilians. We now have a new operation which is focused exclusively on our base."

Sue remembered SLINGSHOT from her earlier in her tour in Cyprus. It was a joint UK-US operation to disrupt efforts to deliver advanced improvised explosive device (IED) materials from Europe to terrorists in Iraq. This was the first piece of the network that led to uncovering a Russian mafia connection with the sale and delivery of advanced technologies. MACE, where the MIKEs and George's team had first worked together, was the program completed the past summer to destroy a terrorist network focused on building radiological weapons. The base commander continued, "During these operations, we have uncovered a trove of material which demonstrate links between a transnational criminal enterprise and both Sunni and Shia extremists. The intelligence is now pointing to an attack on RAF Akrotiri and possibly the USAF base in Ramstein, Germany. COBRA has given our operations to counter these threats the code name GAMBIT."

Sue hadn't focused on the data acquired during the summer work on MACE. Most of the data collection had involved exploitation of electronics, especially computers or phones and Sue left that sort of work to the computer geniuses like her colleagues inside the SOF intelligence cell known by it's Ft. Bragg address, Warehouse 171. She hadn't paid much attention to what 171 analyst Flash Billings and Sue's former classmate from the CIA Farm, Melissa Nez, pulled out of the computers. After MACE, she had returned to Cyprus and returned to her regular agent operations. Clearly, there was more to this problem than Sue had imagined.

"We are meeting here today to discuss an initial way forward together. If it turns out that we are looking at a confirmed threat to Ramstein, then we will have to include our German allies. For now, I and my colleagues believe we need to keep this inside our current team. With that brief introduction, I will turn this over to Squadron Leader Maxwell who has been building the threat analysis for us here at Akrotiri."

"Thank you, sir. I want to begin with a brief background for the entire team…"

Two hours later, Sue stumbled out of the conference room with Jameson on the scheduled 15-minute break. "Chief, remind me next time to shoot myself first so I don't have to suffer through another briefing like that."

"Hey. It wasn't so bad. I did lose count when we got to slide 150 in the Agency PowerPoint." Jameson shook his head and said, "I don't know what is worse, fighting terrorists or living through the bureaucracy of joint counterterrorism operations."

"Easy. Bureaucracy." Sue hadn't realized that Patty Dentmann had come up behind them.

"Chief, we weren't talking about you."

"Actually, Sue, you were talking about me and the rest of the seniors in the room. Now you have seen the sausage factory, do you still want the meal?"

"I certainly do." Jameson was doing his best to share the blame for their comments.

"We have another two hours yet to go. Let me give you a short version of what we are going to do."

"We?" Jameson appeared honestly puzzled.

"Yes, we, Mr. Jameson." Dentmann continued. "My station has a pair of CT sources that augment the two sources Ms. O'Connell still has on her books. We are going to task all four sources to get as close as possible to the al Qaida cell that the geniuses in London and Washington have identified as threatening Akrotiri. Sue, given the fact that your sources are all associated with smuggling, I expect yours will have better access to what we want. The S&R capability," Dentmann paused and stared directly into Jameson's eyes, "that's your side of the equation. It will help on two fronts. First, to keep all the case officers safe and, then, to find and fix the AQ cell once we get closer to the source. After that, I think the SBS team takes over. It is RAF Akrotiri after all. SBS commander is sending down another section from George's team, so there will be plenty of guns available. Now, Mr. Jameson. I hope you don't mind working with O'Connell again. "

"No, ma'am. So, now that we know what we are going to do, does that mean we don't have to go back for the rest of the briefing?"

Dentmann laughed a loud and rather rude laugh that ended in a snort, "No, it just means you can start thinking about your part of the mission instead of just playing with your pencil and rolling your eyes."

"Chief, I did not do that in the briefing."

"Oh, yes, you did." Sue couldn't help enjoying this back and forth, but she wasn't all that pleased that she was going to have to return to the briefing. After some months away from Cyprus, she needed to get back to her files and then get out on the street and set up meetings with her two intelligence sources in Cyprus: Code numerals 206 and 207.

Sue was sitting at one end of the shipping container holding a cup of coffee. Jameson, Billy and George from S&R were perched on the tables that normally held Sue's commo equipment and maps. George, the SBS team leader was sitting on a folding chair he brought from his container located on the other side of the aircraft hanger. They were all dressed in European style casual clothes. Sue was working through the agent meeting plan for the evening. It would be a car pickup. There was a map of the Limassol port with an enlargement of the docks area. On the map were a series of Post It papers with colors and numbers on major intersections. They would use these as map references as needed while on the street.

"Easy enough, guys," Sue said. "I honestly don't think I need you for 207 CPU, but the COS was pretty insistent that the team covers any of our meetings."

"Well, can you blame her? There is the point that the last time you had an agent meeting here, you ended up in the trunk of a car that was wired as an IED." Two years ago, Billy's tone would have meant the comment was a criticism. After a few years on the team, it was just an effort to ease the tension.

"Billy, you say that as if it was a bad thing." SBS team leader George added to the joke.

"OK, so here's the deal" Sue brought the chatter back to the work at hand. "You have a beacon on my car, and Billy checked it again today. It means that you can work a two vehicle cover at a fair distance. Chief, I defer to you if you want to use the Magic Bus tonight or not."

"I think we need to," Jameson said. "The radio and mobile intercept bubble we can create will help us identify the comms of any known bad guys. The station provided us with a list of targeted mobiles and George loaded them into the computers inside the Bus. Since he and Billy are the smart guys, they get to run the Bus tonight."

Jameson turned to British George with a smile and added, "My George gets to ride in the back." He knew that even if you weren't susceptible to motion sickness, riding in the back of a blacked-out mini-bus staring at computers and radio monitors was not exactly the most enjoyable way to make a living. "I get to drive the new Vectra. Sue, do what you can to make the meeting short. I know our George really really hates riding in the vomit comet."

"Trust me, I will make it as short as possible," Sue said. "I'm just here to collect whatever 207 delivers based on the tasking from last week. It's not like I enjoy driving around the docks, listening to him, trying to write down key points, steer and shift left handed. "

Jameson put on the serious face and they all paid attention.

"Listen, all of you. We've now worked through two of Sue's meetings and two of the station's meetings in the past 10 days with no drama. That doesn't mean that every meeting is going to be simple. We are here because the COS believes there is a threat to Sue and her assets. Our job is to identify any potential threat before it becomes a real threat so we can let Sue know to abort the meeting or to get clear of the area, ditch 207 and then get back to base. Check?"

"Check."

"OK, Sue. Give us your planned route into the car pickup site, your planned route while you are debriefing 207, and your route back to base."

It took Sue about 10 minutes to give her guardian angels the routes turn by turn and her assessment of the possible obstacles, likely security risks, and her planned abort route should anything happen. Billy and Jameson then gave her their planned routes. They finished off by confirming the time they would mount up in their vehicles. SBS George took notes to ensure that his team would know precisely where the action was if at any time they needed to serve as the quick reaction force..

After the formal side of the briefing, the four Americans went through an equipment check. They were already wearing lightweight body armor under their shirts. The armor had Velcro covered pockets on both sides under their armpits. On the right side, the standard S&R encrypted radio fit tight into a pocket. On the left side, a Glock 19 pistol in a deep concealment. Sue would not wear her pistol in the S&R rig. She had a concealment holster with her Glock 26 compact pistol attached to the driver's door side of her car seat . She also had a small surefire flashlight in a holster on the inside of her right leg. If she had to fight inside the car, the pistol might be too difficult to put into action. They all carried small Surefire flashlights with enough lumination to destroy anyone's night vision. Sue was convinced she could also use the flashlight as a blunt force weapon after she blinded the individual. As a final step, Sue pulled the small neck knife over her head. As Jameson had told her when he gave it to her "Never leave home without it." It was more of a talisman than a weapon, but in the special operations trade, a talisman often seemed useful enough. They walked to the vehicles.

Sue picked from her three available vehicles a Fiat 500 right hand drive for this meeting. The 500 was small, fast and had several modifications, including a turbo-charged engine and better tires. It also had four rally headlamps mounted on a front crash bar. While it wasn't exactly a normal car on the street, there were enough young rally and "wanna be" rally racers in Cyprus that it fit in well enough. The lights were often referred to as "the blinders" because a flip of the switch transformed the front lights from dim little yellow lanterns to lights that would easily double for aircraft landing lights. The S&R vehicles had "blinders" front and rear, built into the bumpers. They also had modifications to allow the driver to dispatch tear gas and smoke grenades from the front and rear of the car. Not ideal, but much better than trying to use firearms to get clear of a hasty ambush.

Once they got to their vehicles, they checked communications: first internally and then Jameson checked with the SBS team, which would stay on the base but would be prepared to crash out quickly. Jameson used his team leader call sign of Zero and started the check with *"All stations, this is Zero. Radio check."*

"Zero, this is Mike4. Commo check." Sue remained quite fond of her call sign from S&R and was glad to be using it again with Jameson.

"4, Zero, check."

"Zero, Mike8," George already sounded forlorn as he called in from the back of the Magic Bus.

"8, Zero, check."

"Zero, Mike3," While Billy didn't need to call in from the Magic Bus, since George would be covering his comms while he drove, it was standard procedure to confirm all communications. As Jameson always said, "In SOF, team success and safety means we all work for the Department of Redundancy Department."

"Jack6, Zero," SBS George's voice came on stronger than everyone else since he was currently transmitting from a very powerful antenna system on the top of the hanger.

"Zero, 6 check."

George continued, *"Stay safe out there. We have a game of Monopoly going tonight and don't want to be disturbed."*

"Roger, 6. We will do our best." Jameson was not one for radio humor, but Sue certainly had a laugh as she drove toward one of the rear gates of RAF Akrotiri. By the time she was on the main road headed to Limassol, she was focused on the route and what she would say to 207. She called out the checkpoints as she ran through them through-out her one-hour route. By the time Sue was 20 minutes into the route, she could no longer see any headlights in her rear-view mirror. Like all good guardian angels, Sue's were invisible.

Sue drove the Fiat car through the streets near the port of Limas-sol. The port itself and nearby areas were well lit by street lights designed to help heavy truck drivers find the right place to pick up or drop off their cargo. The street lamps provided a flat white light that was excellent for driving but created a flat background of gray shadows along the sides of the street. The Fiat's headlights didn't help much. Right now, she wished she could use the blinders to find 207 in the shadows. As she approached the pickup site, she looked at the dashboard clock. It had just clicked over to 2112hrs. On time and she hoped that 207 was as well.

Sue's stomach was in knots. This was the time when either an operation worked or it didn't. It was also the time when a security service or a terrorist organization would execute an ambush. Instead, 207 stepped out of the shadows approximately 100 feet from the agreed upon meeting place. Sue pulled the car over to the side, unlocked the door and 207 got in. The Fiat's internal lighting had been modified so that the dome light in the car only came on if and when Sue wanted it to do so.

"My friend. Thank you for meeting tonight."

"It is as we agreed."

"Mustafa, it is still important, and I appreciate your work."

"I don't have much time tonight, so can I tell you what I know and leave?"

"What is the problem?"

"No problems, I just have work to do for the Port and I need to get back to work."

"At this hour of the night?"

"Enough. Please, let me tell you what I know and then I can go."

Sue was already beginning to feel uncomfortable. 207 had always been very businesslike, but something was not right. She looked in her rear-view mirror as she turned away from the port and headed into Limassol. Her plan was to drive no more than 10 minutes with 207 in the car, but this sounded like he wanted out, and now. Sue had worked up several contact codes with Jameson and the team over the past few days. She used the microphone switch located on her right hip next to her pistol to click three dots on their internal comms. This was their agreed upon code. Morse code for S; S for Standby. As with the actual word "standby" in the surveillance world, it meant that there was something out there.

In Sue's earbud, Jameson's calm voice said *"Check, 4. 8, you got anything on the radar?"*

"Zero, 8. Nothing. All clear."

"4, Zero. Nothing from our side. You have something going on in the car?"

Sue replied with dot dash dot: Morse for R; R for Roger.

"4, Zero. Confirm, something in the car. 8, I will be closing in to 300m. 4 is away from the port, so it will fit with the traffic."

"Zero, 8. Roger."

"Zero, Jack6. Anything needed from our side?"

"6, so far, so good. I will let you know if you need to go to standby."

"Roger, Zero. 6, out."

With that exchange, Sue relaxed some and returned her attention to 207. He was used to pauses like this in car meetings. Sometimes, the debriefer had to focus on driving.

"Mustafa, what is it you need to tell me."

"I have a manifest that I want to give you. It shows a ship coming in tomorrow night. The *Carras Cargo*. There are eight crew and one passenger. It does not look right. The ship is coming from Alexandria, stopping here but not offloading any cargo. I have never seen a passenger on this ship. It is a cargo ship and the eight crew members have always been the same. This time, there are nine crew. A new man named Ibrahim Meshki. No records on him. I do not like it." He handed the paper to Sue.

"Thank you. Why are you so nervous, Mustafa?"

"The Hizballahis. They are asking questions. They know something."

Sue tried to remain calm as she asked, "What?"

"I do not know what. What do you think?" He looked pale in the dashboard light.

"Do you want my help leaving town? Do you need to get out of town for a while?"

"They have warned me not to leave. They have found my cousin in Beirut and another in Gaza. They warned me to keep faithful or I would pay and my cousins would pay. "

"It this ship one of the Hizballahis' cargo ships?"

"No. Theirs is coming next week. I don't have the details yet. They will load cargo and go in one night. It is an arms shipment, I think. I do not know. The *Carras Cargo* ship, it is not Hizballahi. Perhaps coming from the Arabian Gulf. I don't know."

"Is it a large cargo offload for them?"

"I just said, I do not know." His voice was more strained. Sue realized this was not going to go well if she didn't change the subject.

"OK, Mustafa. Do not worry. If there is something you need to tell me, you know how to contact me. The phone number is always there. We will set our next meeting for well after the cargo shipment. We are playing a long game here, we don't need to know immediately about every shipment. But this news on the passenger, this is important. Thank you." She used her left hand to reach between her seat and the center console. She pulled out an envelope with his salary.

207 took the envelope, pocketed it, and fidgeted in his seat. Usually, this was the time when they focused on small talk and more on his own background while she got him back to the port. Sue could tell she wasn't going to get much more out of him.

"Mustafa, I need you to do something more for me."

"Momken." Perhaps in Arabic. Sometimes it really meant perhaps, sometimes it meant "no way." At this point, Sue wasn't sure which meaning was the most likely.

"I would like you to phone the number you have tomorrow and the next day until the Carras has left port. Can you do that?" Sue's predecessor on Cyprus, Dave Daniels, had given 207 a non-attributable mobile phone and kept a similar phone. It would be fine for a pretext call. All 207 had to do was call as if pre-ordering from a takeout menu from a Limassol restaurant. Lebanese food order was a sign of life and meant all was well. Italian food meant he wanted an emergency meeting – most probably for extraction. The current context would fit either.

"What time?"

"Anytime. I just want to know you are ok."

"Inshallah." Not a huge level of agreement. Inshallah meant God Willing, but sometimes it meant "maybe if I want to," sometimes it meant "I hope so" and sometimes it meant "no." Again, Sue wasn't sure what it meant this time.

"Can I drop you off outside of the port? Can you get a taxi?"

"Yes, yes. Just let me off at the next street near that café."

Sue looked down the street. About five blocks ahead was a small coffee shop catering to dockworkers. It looked safe enough. No parked cars and no loitering strangers. She committed and turned left into a dark street and pulled over. She was two blocks from the café.

"Safe travels." Mustafa said this as he was leaving. He closed the door and walked into the darkness.

Sue was not happy about their farewell. She checked her mirrors and pulled away from the curb. She made a right turn against traffic at the next available intersection and started a stair step away from the drop off point. She keyed the mike and said, *"Zero, 4"*

"4, go."

"Drop off complete. RTB."

"Roger. All, 4 returning to base."

"Stand by, stand by." George's voice came on the air, stronger than the others because of the antennas in the Magic Bus.

"8, Zero. Go ahead."

"Zero, there was mobile activity as soon as 4 dropped off 207 and cleared that street and headed back toward the main. It looks like two cars waiting on cross streets about three blocks from the drop off. Two different phones from the list we got from station. I'm using GSM to track right now. Looks like they are right on top of 4. Any chance 207 knew where he was going to be dropped off?"

"8, 4. Not that I could figure. I just ran the normal..." Sue realized that she had violated one of the rules of espionage: never use the same route with the same agent more than once. The pattern she had used with 207 was precisely the same as the last meeting. While focused on his demeanor and his worries, she had just gone on autopilot and had taken a comfortable route that used the streets to circle around the port. If they were blocks away from the drop off point, they may not have seen 207. They may have been waiting based on her previous route. Or, they may have flipped 207 already and he gave them the site. A small error and suddenly Sue couldn't say anything for sure except one thing. "He picked the drop off point."

"4, Zero. We have your beacon, we know where you are. 8 will lock on the GSM signals. Take the next left turn and run that street until I say otherwise. 8, Zero. Track those mobiles. Are they closing on 4?"

"Zero, negative. They appear to be trailing 4 about a half mile back, but we only have one turn so far. Must be in two different Charlies." As they moved into "operational mode", George had switched to S&R shorthand. Alphas were places, Bravos were people, Charlies were vehicles.

"4, you keep on your route for now. I want you to take a right across traffic at MUSTANG, then a left at CAMARO, and proceed on that route until instructed. 3, use the beacon and run an intercept route to get in front of 4. Our

goal is to intercept 4 at DAYTONA. I will close from the rear. By that time, we should be able to determine if this is surveillance." Jameson was using their newly established map checkpoints. Sometimes the checkpoints were named cities, sometimes, states. On this trip, Jameson decided to use sports cars. DAYTONA was on the main highway on the way to Akrotiri.

"*Roger.*" Billy's voice was filled with adrenaline. Sue was convinced her voice would be as well when next asked to talk. She took a couple of deep breaths to clear some of the adrenaline, but not all of it, out of her system. She took the left turn and started North away from the port and toward the city center. Her most likely route back to base would be another left turn about a mile ahead. She could see car headlights closing from behind. She was a quarter mile from the right turn at checkpoint *MUSTANG.* She took another breath.

"*Zero, 4.*"

"*Go.*"

"*You closing in on me?*"

"*Not me, 4. Take that right at MUSTANG, then the left turn at CAMARO. Copy?*"

Sue exhaled and started to relax a bit. If it had been an ambush, it would likely have already happened. The plan now was to use the team to determine if it was surveillance or coincidence. Once that was determined, she would be on her way home and there was all the chance in the world that all of this was simply nerves. She reached the intersection and took the right crossing traffic. It gave her a chance to glance back at the traffic behind her. She couldn't determine which one was the vehicle that George was tracking.

"*Stand by, stand by.*" George again.

"*8, Zero.*"

"*Another mobile just joined the conversation. This time, it is in front of 4 at Hot Rod.*"

"*Roger, 8. We have three linked mobiles – one in front of 4 and two behind 4.*"

"*Correct, Zero.*"

Sue was not pleased by this. A team that was in front of her and behind her could control her travel for whatever purpose they chose – surveillance or ambush.

"All, Zero." Jameson was calling for everyone to pay attention.

"4"

"8"

"3"

"I think I am behind the parade following 4. 8 confirm."

"Roger, Zero. There should be two Charlies in front of you."

"Roger, 8. First Charlie – mid 90s Mercedes C class. Black. Lights around the license plate are out, so I can't cover the numbers. Second Charlie closest to me is a dark Peugeot 205 – 2002 or 2003. Cyprus plates M305YY, M305YY. Looks like two in the Peugeot. At least two if not more in the Mercedes. OK, Mercedes is now Charlie 1, Peugeot is Charlie 2. Confirm."

Sue took a breath and confirmed she heard the transmission. The rest of the team did the same.

"4, take the next left at Hot Rod not repeat not at CAMARO, confirm."

"Roger, left at Hot Rod."

"3, Zero. Can you work up an intercept route once 4 is on the main?"

"Roger, Zero. I can still intercept at DAYTONA. Where in the parade do you want me?"

"3, get in front of 4. I want you between 4 and Charlie 3. I want eyes on Charlie 3."

"Roger." Billy didn't release the mike key for a few seconds. Sue could hear the engine of the Magic Bus fighting to accelerate.

"4, I want you to slow down gradually – no brakes, just downshift. I need the show to slow down a bit, so I can pass Charlie 1 and 2."

Sue took her foot slowly off the accelerator pedal, let the RPMs slow, downshifted into third gear. Speed shifting with her prosthetic foot had always been a challenge, but she was managing just fine at this point. Her Fiat slowed. She could see the two Charlies struggling to keep their distance as she changed speed. She remembered her instructors pointing out that while movies emphasized car chases and acceleration, the best way to determine surveillance was to reduce speed gradually and see if anyone maintained the precise gap from you. Of course, a good surveillance team like S&R will respond not by mirroring your pace but passing you, getting out in front and shifting cars so that a new team takes over the position behind the target. Either these guys didn't have enough manpower to do that or they were determined to follow Sue until some ambush point and didn't really care if Sue knew they were there.

"4, accelerate." Jameson's voice remained calm. Sue downshifted into second gear and gunned the little Fiat. She was surprised when the car seemed to jump forward; she felt the turbocharger engage before she heard its whine. The gap between her car and the Charlies increased dramatically. Sue looked in her rear-view mirror and saw Jameson's Vectra. Just as he pulled out, he turned on his "blinders" under his front bumper as he went by. Sue knew the drill, so she had angled the rear-view mirror away from her. Whatever was going to happen behind her was going to happen and seeing it wasn't going to help.

Once Jameson turned on the high performance light bar, anyone in the two Charlies would be hard pressed to keep their night vision. Jameson shut off the front blinders and tucked his vehicle neatly behind Sue with about a foot to spare between his bumper and her rear bumper. He then turned on the rear blinders. Sue was certain she saw the two Charlies swerve responding to the flash of light from Jameson. If Jameson was following their practice, he would then throw the switch that shut off all the lights to the rear of his vehicle. To anyone trailing, the transition from bright light to no light would feel like they had just fallen into a cave.

"You can accelerate now." No official commo talk. Just a quiet Jameson voice. Jameson had always been the team dad since the beginning of the MIKEs and like a good father, he worked hard to stay calm no matter what happened. For sure, it made Sue calm down. She downshifted again and pushed the Fiat as hard as she could first in second gear and then third and fourth. Jameson stayed right behind her as they left the two trailing Charlies behind.

"8, Zero. Where is Charlie 3?"

"Zero, about a half mile in front of you on the parallel street, but you are closing, fast."

"Roger. 4, take the next left. Take it at speed."

"Roger."

"3 and 8, you need to recalculate the intercept route."

"Roger, Zero. With this turn, we will intercept at the MONZA intersection not DAYTONA."

Sue made the 90 degree turn at 40 mph and just barely controlled the move as she down shifted and accelerated through the turn. During selection, her driving instructor had said, "You can do three things with a car: turn, accelerate or brake. Do everything you can to do them one at a time because if you try to do two out of the three, you will not succeed." Luckily, no one was in the left lane as she skidded through the turn and then accelerated. Jameson followd her in the Vectra. The two Charlies tried to keep up by going into the turn at full speed. The first Charlie misjudged the turn and ran up on the left side curb and rubbed his front tire against a street light. At speed, Jameson had hoped it just might bend a wheel rim or flatten a tire. Indeed, the Mercedes fell behind and then stopped.

Once again the calm voice of Jameson, *"OK, 4. Accelerate as much as that Fiat will take it. I don't want you to blow the engine, but..."*

"Check, boss." Sue was already keeping track of the red line on the RPM dial. She was running in fourth gear at 5000 RPM racing through the outskirts of Limassol at nearly 80mph. Unsafe speed in the dark, but orders were orders.

"8, we are closing on MONZA."

"Roger. We are in place. As soon as we see your lights, we will join you."

Again, Jameson's voice on the net said, *"Where is Charlie 3?"*

George's voice was strained. *"He doesn't appear to have handled your last turn all that well. I show him trying to get back in trail."*

"Here we come." Sue saw Billy accelerate the Magic Bus into the highway. He was going 70mph halfway through the turn entering the highway. All Sue could think was "poor George." Riding in the Magic Bus was never fun. At these speeds it would be ugly.

"4, 3"

"Go, 3." Sue tried to sound calm. She was certain she didn't.

"Turn the blinders off, please."

Sue hadn't realized she had switched on the blinders as soon as she accelerated back at MONZA. It couldn't have been pleasant for Billy as he pulled in front. She switched off the LED lights and it appeared for a moment as if the world had gone completely dark.

Finally, she picked up the rear of the Magic Bus in her pathetic yellow headlamps.

"Thank you. Zero, RTB?"

"Roger. RTB."

"Check." As they got closer to RAF Akrotiri, they lost Charlie 1 and according to George, Charlie 3 never did catch up.

As they entered their official gate to RAF Akrotiri, Sue noticed the RAF military policeman doing a double take as he saw how close and how fast they drove to the gate. George had used the onboard radio to call ahead so they didn't have to go through a formal check, but that didn't mean the MP wouldn't check them out. He knew all of them, so it was a cursory check. She also noticed that he did a double take when Jameson drove by. Sue pulled into the hanger, parked the Fiat and got out. She was unsteady on her feet. Partly due to several hours in a less than ideal bucket seat, but partly due to the adrenaline washing out of her system. She looked at the Fiat. It would need new tires and it wasn't entirely certain that the engine wasn't right on the edge of sending a rod through the engine block. Still, it did its job.

"Won't pass any sergeant major inspection now." Once he knew they were returning to the airbase, SBS George had changed into his "off duty" kit: black shorts, tan t-shirt, flip flops.

"Guess not."

Jameson pulled up and got out of his car. Sue noticed there was a crease in his roofline that ran from the right rear to the right front. More of a long dent than anything else.

"What's that?"

"Fan mail. They really didn't like me passing them." He ran his hand along the length of the roof.

"I didn't see a muzzle flash."

"I didn't either, but then I was kinda busy."

Billy parked the Magic Bus and got out. He walked by the Vectra. "It's a nice look, but that's gonna' reduce the resale value. SRR in Iraq is going to be pissed.." He kept on walking.

Jameson turned to both of them.

"OK, let's get our kit out of the vehicles and do a quick debriefing.

Clearly, we have to get some of this story to the base commander and to Nicosia."

"Tomorrow?" Sue was not looking forward to waking up either the base commander or the COS.

"Tonight. There are going to be watch commanders here and probably a watch officer at station. We send it to them. They decide if they wake up the Air Commodore or the COS. After that, we regroup tomorrow early and do a full debriefing, plus pass whatever intel you got from 207 to higher."

"Check."

Billy was walking away from the van. He turned to Sue.

"You might want to help our George. I think he is really feeling poorly."

Sue opened the sliding door of the van. "Enjoy the ride?"

"Ever so much, thank you." Sue had never seen a man whose face was well and truly green. Even when paratroopers in aircraft started to get airsick, it was usually a 'one and done' sort of upset. George looked like he was going to take a while to recover.

"Boss says we have to do a debrief."

"I know. It is going to take me a minute or so to get my focus back."

"Yup. Billy likes driving the Magic Bus."

The morning briefing had resulted in action on all fronts. Dentmann and the Military Attaché told the attendees on the video teleconference that they would fly down from Nicosia. The Air Commodore gave the SBS team the warning order to prepare for a takedown operation, targets and venue to be determined. The S&R crew were already preparing to cover Meshki as soon as his feet left the gangway and hit the docks. Sue was left with precious little to do except coordinate between her US and UK pals. That all changed when Dentmann arrived on the military attaché's Beechcraft 300. Sue had heard about people who sucked the air out of the room when they walked in. For all of her five-foot-nothing frame, Dentmann was one of those people. The Air Commodore was certainly captured.

"OK, there are several questions that we don't have answered and I'm not happy about it." Dentmann opened with this statement and everyone in the room was immediately unhappy as well.

"O'Connell, tell me again what 207 said."

"Meshki is transiting Cyprus on the *Carras Cargo*. Its last port of call was Alexandria and it is bound for Split. 207 was convinced that Meshki was getting off here and that was the reason why the ship was docking."

"Is it something he thinks or something he knows?"

Sue had a sinking feeling in her gut. She didn't have a clue. "Don't know, Chief."

Dentmann frowned and everyone was worried. "OK, that would have been important, but it is not critical. After all, if we get surveillance on the slip where the ship is parking, we can see for ourselves if

Meshki is getting off." She turned to the S&R team. "Mr. Jameson, you have enough resources to pull this off?"

"Chief, we have the manpower. We will get long-range eyes on as best we can and if the Bravo leaves the ship, we will have him under control."

"Excellent. Now for the surveillance from last night. What do you make of this, Sue?"

"Chief, I don't honestly know what to make of it. They were clearly surveilling me. According to the Magic Bus readout, they weren't near the drop off point. Rather, they were set up to pick me up once I left the dockyards. I don't know if they intended harm to any of us." Sue recognized that she was caught in another moment where she was talking about what she thought not what she knew.

Dentmann frowned and said "I think Mr. Jameson's car argues that they did. After our previous encounter with the Russians, I suspect we are playing three-dimensional chess right now and don't know our opponent."

Jameson answered, "Roger that, chief."

"OK, Mr. Jameson, your team had this covered. What do you think?"

"Chief, I think they were after Sue, they knew her pattern and they knew she had a meeting in the dockyards. Otherwise, they would have set up someplace closer to the airbase. I don't know if that is because they surveilled 207 to the pickup and locked on to Sue afterwards, or if they were after Sue from the beginning."

"Well, this is a puzzlement." The Air Commodore was baffled and it was clear that he allowed his "inside voice" to run out his mouth.

Dentmann broke up the pause, "OK, so we can at least consider the possibility that 207 was not part of the surveillance equation. Air Commodore, I recommend we shelve this conundrum for the time being and focus on Meshki and his potential threat to your base. With your permission, I can get half a dozen tech officers to come to investigate this...after we sort out Meshki."

The Air Commodore was back in charge and he was clearly in his comfort zone. "SBS, are you ready? Do you need anything from me?"

George responded, "Sir, if we could have a helo standing by, ideally a Gazelle little bird, it might be very useful depending on where we are going tonight."

"Done."

"Mr. Jameson, what do you need?"

"Sir, we are ready. I don't suppose you have any access points to warehouses inside the port?"

"Sadly, no," The commodore looked at Dentmann.

"Mr. Jameson, we have a warehouse near the port. It won't help getting eyes on, but it will serve as a good staging area."

"Perfect, chief. How soon and where do I get the keys?"

Dentmann slid them across the table showing everyone at the table that she was working several steps ahead of them. The key ring had a small tag on it with an address. "Alarm code is 42416."

Jameson smiled and said, "Thanks, chief."

Dentmann turned back to the Air Commodore. His room, his base, his agenda – more or less. The Air Commodore took his cue. "OK, ladies and gentlemen, I think we have plenty to do before the *Carras Cargo* arrives. I have one of our surveillance aircraft tracking the ship right now. Unless there is a major change, we expect the ship to enter the docks at 2215hrs tonight. I will keep you informed if there are any changes. Off you go," the Air Commodore stood up, gestured to Dentmann to leave the room with him. Once they were gone, the teams continued to work the plan for another hour and then called it enough, left the building and went back to the hanger.

The MILATT stopped Sue before she could join the rest of the gang. "Colonel Williams, what can I do for you," Sue switched to military precision. Jack Williams was nominally her boss in country, a friend of her real boss from 171, Colonel Jed Smith, and definitely a friend of the COS. He had serious juice in country for a military officer and she didn't want to be on his bad side.

"Sue, relax. I just needed to give you some background Patty wanted you to know. She expected the Air Commodore would take her to the Officer's Mess as soon as the meeting was over and she left me to serve as the messenger."

"Check, sir. Where do you want to go."

"Brody is over there in the suburban. I think that works. I also understand he has a thermos of black coffee in case you want something."

"Coffee will be great." One of the rules from the FARM, if you are offered something to drink or something to eat, take it. This was a follow up to the first rule for a case officer, always pee when you can. They arrived at the Suburban and Brody already had two cups of very hot, very strong coffee waiting.

"Good to see you again, Chief."

"Thanks, Brody. And thanks for the coffee."

"After any meeting with a senior, I know I always need a cup." Brody looked at Williams and Williams nodded.

"So, here is something to consider. The station has an asset who also fingered Meshki as part of the threat to the Base, so this is definitely a hot one. We can expect to get something tonight. Dentmann wants you to be the lead interrogator for the initial set of questions at the base. Eventually, he is going to be sent somewhere not so nice, depending on his nationality of course. We will need to get information out of him well before he makes that trip."

"Sir, I don't want to sound unreasonable, but why me?"

"Because, Chief O'Connell, the COS has asked you to do it and what Dentmann wants, Dentmann gets. Clear?"

"Check, sir."

"Personally, I think she wants to give you something to do so that you don't go out on the street tonight and create an international incident." Williams was smiling when he said that, but only a little bit of a smile. Brody started the Suburban and drove back to the hanger. He dropped Sue off and then drove back to main headquarters of RAF Akrotiri. No telling if Williams was going home tonight with Brody or not. Sue suspected not.

Sue was sitting in the Magic Bus, responsible for playing "Zero" tonight. Nate was doing the needful driving the bus – slowly circling around the port and the associated streets of Limassol. This would give the S&R team the maximum number of surveillance operators on the street. Plus, since Sue knew all of the players in the operation, both Jameson and George wanted her voice on the command channel. Everyone back at Akrotiri agreed. However, they insisted on monitoring all channels from base operations.

"All call signs, Zero, the time is 2030hrs, radio check."

"Mike6," Jameson was in the Vectra approximately a mile away just outside the port entrance.

"Mike8," S&R George was in a newly rented Peugeot parked near one of the main truck gates that was still open.

"Mike2," Joe was on foot next to one of the warehouses near the slip where the *Carras Cargo* would dock. He was going to be the primary eye on target.

"Mike5," Billy was on the opposite side of the slip. He could parallel any foot traffic and remain invisible among the shipping containers.

"Mike3," Deke was in another rental, a Ford Fiesta, next to the other main truck gate.

Assuming Meshki, now called Bravo1, would arrive and hold a meeting, Billy and Joe would be responsible for the initial eyes on, then match up with two of the vehicles. They would then run "two up" in the trail of the third S&R vehicle which would follow Bravo1. That was assuming he was picked up in a vehicle. On Sue's chart in the Magic Bus, this unknown vehicle was already named Charlie1. If he didn't get picked up, they would follow him on foot until he either got a cab or went to his bed down location. The BDL was yet to be identified, but it was already named on the chart in front of Sue as Alpha1. It was dark, the port facility was large and no one thought it would be an easy run tonight.

As Jameson said before they left, "If it was easy, we would let the Klingons do it." Sue winced. Klingons in SOF parlance was a way to describe agent handlers like Sue, but more often, CIA handlers. It was all about implying handlers used "cloaking devices." As the daughter and granddaughter of CIA officers, she had heard the joke so many times, it was no longer amusing.

"Jack 6." The SBS team was still inside RAF Akrotiri waiting in their Land Rovers. It made no sense to preposition them since no one knew where the Bravo would take them. If he went too far afield, George and his team would load up in a helo and arrive at the destination by air instead of by ground.

"Zero, Akrotiri6." The base commander was determined to be the on-site commander. At this point, mostly what that meant was calling the first, the middle and the last shots. Arrival of the ship, launching the SBS team, and clearing the site for exploitation by the S&R team. *"Surveillance aircraft has identified target approaching the slip."*

Silence while two pairs of eyes watched the ship come into the dock and two dozen sets of ears waited to hear the operation unfold.

"Stand by, stand by. Mike2. We have a Bravo coming down the gangway. He has a full size aluminum roller case. No other passengers coming off the ship. It looks like the ship came into dock just to drop him off. They are pulling up the gangway. I have the Bravo."

"All, Zero. Mike2 has our Bravo on foot with an aluminum case."

"Zero, 5. Paralleling through the containers.

"Roger, 2 has the eye and 5 is running parallel."

They walked along the docks until Bravo1 came to the truck entrance. *"Stand by, stand by. Bravo1 was just picked up by a mid 90s black Mercedes. I didn't get the plates. Who can?"* Joe was asking for assistance since he couldn't keep up on foot.

"Mike8 can." George had picked up the car and was following. *"Charlie1 is headed away from the port on the main. Currently at Bristol."* The

SBS team had won the argument; map references tonight were British cities.

"Mike3, Zero. Pick up our two guys on foot. Mike6 can you get in trail behind 8?" In front of Sue was a large laminated map of Limassol. She was marking the routes as she transmitted them to the team.

"Zero, 8. Charlie1 at Bristol heading North, North to Newcastle. Speed 30."

"Roger. 6, when can you intercept?"

Jameson came on the net and said, *"6 can at Swindon."*

"Roger. 8 maintain until Swindon. 6 can."

"3, Zero. When can you get in the run?"

"Zero, 3. We can at Worcester or any parallel. We are running parallel at Oxford."

"6 has Charlie1"

"All, 6 has Charlie1. 8, move parallel along your route. 3, find a layup at Oxford," Sue was managing the full team at this point. She knew from experience that Jameson always put at least one car in a layup in case the target tried to double back.

Once again, Jameson called in, *"Charlie1, left, left at Birmingham and entering southbound main. Charlie 1 has reversed course and is now heading South toward Oxford."*

"3, intercept at Oxford"

The mobile in Sue's pocket rang. Sue knew this was 207's call.

"Hello."

"I just wanted you to know I am ordering Lebanese tonight. We are going to stop the Carras Cargo tonight once it anchors out in the harbor."

"We?"

"Of course. Surely you knew, I am a Senior Captain in the Customs Police."

"Mustafa, did you tell my predecessor about your job?"

"Of course." Sue was furious. She always suspected Dave Daniels played fast and loose with his reporting. Now, it was clear that he had chosen not to report 207's affiliation with the Cypriot Security apparatus. Perfect. If Daniels wasn't in the US recovering from his time as a hostage in Syria, she would fly to CONUS and choke him.

"Mustafa, we are working the case on the ground now. I will have to call you back."

"Inshallah."

The surveillance serial lasted another hour with the three cars switching the lead as their target moved in Limassol and finally headed East out of the city in the rural farmland. The vehicle eventually pulled up in front of a farmhouse. Deke deployed Billy and Joe to get eyes on the target and the team vehicles set up stakeout positions along the nearby roads.

"*Zero, 5. Alpha1 is a single story farmhouse with a small barn about 25 meters away. The only signs of life are from Bravo1 and the driver of our Charlie. I have a good layup position with line of sight to the house and the barn. 2 is with me.*"

"*Roger, 5. Jack6, it seems we have our bed down location.*"

"*Zero, Jack6. Roger on the BDL. On our way. We will be in two Defenders. ETA, 30 minutes.*"

A thirty minute stakeout in a rural area can seem like forever. Billy and Joe were fine in their over-watch position, but the cars had to be kept on the move to avoid third party compromise if some farmer called the local constabulary. Sue was getting bored inside the Magic Bus when one of computers alarmed.

Sue said, "*Stand by, stand by. Mobile identified in Charlie3 last night is moving toward our Alpha.*"

"*Zero, Jack6. We are going to slow our arrival to see if the mobile in Charlie3 pulls up at the house.*"

Sue watched the GSM tracker as it approached the farm house.

"*Stand by stand by.*" Billy definitely sounded excited. "*Charlie3 pulled up to the house. Single male, fit. No weapon visible. He's going inside.*"

"*Jack6, you copy?*"

"*Roger. 3 Bravos for sure. Any sign of other life in the house.*"

"*No other signs of life. The house was dark until our first two Bravos arrived.*"

"*All, Jack6. We are one minute out. Be prepared to handle squirters.*" Sue had used the term squirters before with other US raids. These were individuals that might escape the initial raid. She didn't realize it was in the SBS vocabulary as well. Once again, Sue was pissed she wasn't going to see the SBS team at work. Just as she was about to acknowledge the same another of the computer screens in the Magic Bus illuminated.

"Zero, Jack6. Are you receiving our feed from the helmet cameras?"

"Roger."

"Please record same." Sue reached over to the mouse attached to the newly alive computer. She turned on the record function.

The camera was probably mounted on George's helmet. They were in a stack formation with Dozer in the lead with a battering ram and George at the end of the stack. The movement of the camera made the images quirky, but still Sue couldn't tear her eyes off the screen.

George's hand filled the screen. Every SBS head was turned to watch the hand. Four fingers, then three, then two, then one. Dozer's ram hit the door just as George's hand made a fist. The first thing following the ram was a pair of flash bang grenades thrown into the room. The blast blinded the camera for a second then the internal camera chip reset itself for the new light and Sue watched as the SBS team split left and right from the door frame. George pulled to the right following Paddy. Mac and Brian had followed Dozer to the left of the door. The flash bang grenades successfully disoriented the three players in the room such that they never got a chance to pull out any weapons. This saved their lives because any threat would have been handled with a double tap in the chest followed by another round in the head. The three individuals were secured with flex cuffs, hooded, and searched for weapons. Sue watched as George noted two Beretta pistols and a Skorpion machine pistol.

"It would appear that we got the right place." George said with some relief. Sue was equally relieved. After all, up to that point, all they knew for sure was one of their Bravos had gotten off a boat and was meeting two other Bravos outside Limassol. Probably not a good enough excuse to conduct a raid. George walked over to the aluminum case. It was unlocked and open. He turned out his surefire flashlight to illuminate the contents.

"Looks to be approximately 10 kilos of plastic explosive with a wiring harness. Switches and fuses are in a separate box on the side."

A voice appeared suddenly on the net. It was slightly distorted which everyone on the net knew meant that the speaker was in a helicopter.

"All, this is Akrotiri6. Well done. I will arrive with a full team of base police and ordnance disposal personnel in five minutes. Two helos. Please mark an LZ for us. Once we have landed, I recommend you clear the area. We are going to be inviting the locals to join in the success at that point."

"Akrotiri6, Zero. Roger."

George's voice came on the net. This was now a pure UK operation. *"Jack6. Roger, Akrotiri6. What size helos?"*

"Jack6, we have one Westland and one Bell 212."

"Roger, 6. We will have two separate LZs set up for your big bird and your little bird. Broad arrow signal will be for the Westland. Inverted V will be for the 212."

Sue knew that the team had all heard the same exchange, but she confirmed through internal comms. *"All, mission complete. No squirters. They want us to clear the area. Confirm when you launch RTB."* As Sue headed home, she commented to Nate in the front, "Just another quiet night in Cyprus."

Nate said, "And I thought we were on vacation coming here."

S ue recognized the move of the entire team of Warehouse 171 to the US base in Vincenza Italy made sense. That didn't make the move any easier, it just meant that once the full team got settled it could respond more efficiently to the growing requirements for human intelligence (HUMINT) support to operations in Iraq, Afghanistan, Somalia, North Africa, and the Persian Gulf. When Special Operations Forces (SOF) expanded the war beyond hunting Al Qaida in Afghanistan to include a terrorist "man-hunting" effort world-wide, mission planning became progressively more difficult for any unit based at Ft. Bragg. So, Warehouse 171 would be moved to Camp Ederle in Italy and be renamed the Regional Logistics Support Unit (RLSU). The unit would be located on a base which was headquarters for the US Army Africa Command/Southern European Task Force, the 173rd Airborne Brigade, and a range of temporary residents in the conventional and SOF community that supported operations in the Balkans and the Eastern Mediterranean.

Months ago when Sue heard that 171 would soon be moving to Vincenza, she assumed her days of living in Cyprus were over. After all, the reason she was assigned to RAF Akrotiri was to work on operations focused on the Eastern Med and if the entire office was set up a short hop away, there was no good reason to live in a British base. Her boss, Jed Smith, also made it clear that it was time for another of her colleagues to rotate out of a warzone and enjoy the "peace and quiet" of Cyprus. Smith told Sue she was moving as soon as they could get Ginger on the island.

The secure video teleconference yesterday had been simply to sort out the logistics of the entire transfer. It made sense that her discussion would be with the senior NCO for the team, Command Sergeant Major Jim Massoni. Sue had first worked with Massoni when he was the deputy for the MIKEs. In the years since Sue's time with the MIKEs, Massoni was promoted and reassigned to 171, now RLSU. As long as Sue had known Massoni, he had never quite captured how to use the SVTC, so his face always ended up too close to the camera and his voice too loud for the microphone. In short, Jim Massoni's image and voice were distorted. Coupled with the satellite feed and the encryption, Sue had to struggle to understand him. She thought it must be doubly hard for her partners in the field who often were taking the feed while sitting in a makeshift tent in some warzone.

"Sue, I hope we aren't preventing you from raising hell with the SBS guys in the hanger," Massoni started with a grin knowing it was 0030hrs in Cyprus.

"Jim, right after the MIKEs left Akrotiri for Afghanistan, my SBS mates loaded up and are doing another 90 downrange in Iraq. They are in Basra this time so at least they are near the water."

"Always good to periodically dip frogmen into salt water."

"Too true. Now, I know you don't give a hoot about my sleep cycle, but it is after midnight here, so what do I need to know about the plan?"

"We start taking down 171 on 12 March and shipping the equipment to Vincenza. The first bird will be landing next Tuesday at 0700hrs local at Aviano airbase. We need you to get up there pronto and serve as our advanced team. Brain Trust will follow in the second bird which should arrive sometime on Thursday next. Our tech guru Marconi will be the last one out as he wraps all his precious technology and flies out on our last bird." Massoni paused and readjusted his face on the screen. "Sue, sort out the logistics, work with the Air Force OSI guys so that we can get help handling our classified material and see if you can charm the guys from the 173rd to give us a platoon of young paratroopers to help in the move."

"Roger, Jim. I will talk to the MILATT at the embassy and see if there is any hop I can catch tomorrow," Sue had been working with the military attache for over a year and he was a long-standing pal of Jed Smith so it was easy enough to ask.

"We are sending you the full details shortly, but I wanted to be sure you knew that we are moving out smartly on this and I wanted you to do the needful. Clear?"

"Check, Sergeant Major. I am on the job."

Just before the screen went blank, Massoni backed away from the camera so that he finally looked less like a pumpkin head. He said, "Out here."

Inside her shipping container home, Sue closed down her laptop and stood up to stretch. She was in her sweats which doubled as her sleepwear. She looked around the space which was slightly larger than the Airstream travel trailer her parents had in the 1970s and said to herself, "Looks like we are going to part company."

That night, the dream that regularly visits many combat veterans was worse than usual. Normally, the places and the people in Sue's nightmares were easily recognizable. This time, not so much. Sue was walking on a battlefield filled with flaming tanks, collapsed buildings and dead men. It was foggy. The damaged equipment and the burning tanks were all from World War II. The location must be somewhere in Germany. She was in a patrol made up of her informal SOF mentor, Max Creeter in the lead, her father and her grandfather and Sue in trail. Her father looked back at Sue and whispered, "Remember, when we get to the site, you are the primary debriefer. You are the only one of us who speaks Russian."

Sue felt sick. Somehow, she had forgotten to tell them when they started the patrol that she didn't speak Russian. How could she have forgotten something that important? And she didn't have any requirements. What were the questions for the debriefing? Worse still, she wasn't carrying any weapons and was hopping on one leg because she forgot her prosthetic. It was the worst possible combination. What was she thinking?

Just as she reached out to touch her father and confess she was not going to be able to help, there was a loud explosion. Sue watched as Max and her grandfather were lifted off the ground and thrown 10 meters away. Minefield. They had wandered into a minefield. She couldn't see what had happened to Max or her grandfather. They disappeared in the fog. She fell on her wounded knee just as the machine gun fire started. Her father jumped in front of her to protect her from the tracer rounds that Sue could see landing all around her.

"Goodbye, Sue. It's up to you to complete the mission now."

Sue looked up at her father whose face dissolved. Suddenly, she realized she was already in a metal coffin. They were burying her on the battlefield. They hadn't checked to see if she was alive or dead. Sue could hear the dirt landing on the lid of the coffin. She tried to scream but no sound came out.

Sue woke from the dream, sweat-soaked and crying. Weeks after her first confrontation with the Russian Mafia operator, Nicolai Beroslav, when he locked her in a trunk of a car loaded with explosives, Massoni had as close to a heart-to-heart as he ever had with anyone. He told Sue that it was bad enough that she lost a leg in combat. Now, she had to live with the classic terror of being buried alive. He told her to fly up to the US Air Force base in Aviano and find a military shrink. And then, make regular trips to talk. Massoni didn't reveal much about his own issues. He did say with a knowing smirk that a shrink probably couldn't eliminate the nightmares, but might help make them less frequent. He said, even though SOF raid teams faced death more often conventional Army troops, they didn't have anywhere near the number of PTSD suicides. Massoni said there were always team psychologists available on site as part of the post-operation debriefing. He admitted a shrink had saved his sanity at least once in his 24 years in service.

Unfortunately, just after she had that conversation with Massoni, another stream of events took over her life, with the MACE operation and the revelation that one of her classmates from Agency training was a traitor. That left no time or energy to fly to Aviano.

She used a set of wet ones to wash away the sweat and, she hoped the nightmare. She said to herself, "I saw plenty of death in Afghanistan working with S&R, why am I suddenly a wreck now that I am working with 171?"

She knew there were no answers. Once the 171 team moved to Italy, maybe she would take Massoni up on his recommendation. Maybe she could even link a visit to CONUS in the effort. She looked in the small mirror hanging from the wall of the shipping container. She finished the box of wipes and opened a new one. Just before she shut off the light, she said to herself, "Sweet dreams, Sue. You will be happy to get an afternoon off before you are off on another TDY."

AN EXCHANGE OF BISHOPS

It was very dark on the streets of Tor Kham as Joe Schultz drove his two door, up-armored Mitsubishi Pajero through streets that were filled with people, animals and very large trucks. None of these locals were about to give way to a visiting 4WD truck no matter how short the wheelbase. The four Rangers in Joe's security detachment were in quad-cab truck behind him and had already made multiple comments in his ear bud trying to describe how dark it was. The winner of the discussion had been "six inches up a cow's ass." Either it was the most accurate description or just grossed out everyone on the security net. Joe noticed that his counter-surveillance team of the MIKEs had been quiet throughout the discussion.

The MIKEs had just returned to Jalalabad after a brief rotation in Cyprus followed by a week R&R at Bragg. It was well known in theatre that the MIKEs' team leader, Bill Jameson, tolerated none of the radio nonsense that was common on the SOF net. Joe came from the SOF raid teams, so he knew that the chatter was simply a way of letting off tension before the operation went down. Given the fact that he was concentrating on his route into the meeting site and reviewing the requirements he would use during the agent meeting, he honestly wished everyone was as quiet as the MIKEs. They were there to ensure he could get in and out of Tor Kham without hostile surveillance on him. Once they pronounced him "clean" of surveillance, he had entered the main part of the city. He didn't need any radio contact with them unless they saw something which pointed to a serious problem. If that happened, they would report the problem and recommend an exfiltration route that Joe and the security team could use to get out of the area.

Joe was scheduled to meet a reporting source with information on terrorists who came across the border from Pakistan, conducted raids on US forces in the area and then crossed back into their safe haven of Pakistan. Joe and his colleague Adam Burkhart were the Eastern Afghanistan team for SOF HUMINT 171. It was their job to find the terrorists, fix them in place in Eastern Afghanistan and let the rest of the SOF shooters finish the job. Joe's guest for tonight's car meeting was Source 524, a military source first recruited in 2002 during the early days of US military operations in Nangarhar province. 524 was a Pakistani citizen, Pashtun smuggler from the Afridi tribe and well connected on both sides of the border. His reporting record was listed back at Bragg as "good to excellent." Joe's primary contact in that brain trust was a 171 analyst known simply as Pluto. Joe was a little embarrassed when he had to admit to the other SOF partners in Jalalabad that he didn't know Pluto's real name since he had never seen him wear anything resembling a uniform. In any event, Pluto made it clear that while 524 might not be a great strategic reporting source on the overall insurgency in Nangarhar, his tactical reporting on smuggling operations, including smuggling terrorists from the Haqqani network and their notorious suicide bombers, was excellent.

The Haqqanis were an Afghan resistance cum criminal network led by Jalaluddin Haqqani, a mujahedin resistance commander in the 1980s and a Taliban cabinet member in the 1990s. After the Taliban were driven out of Kabul, he moved across the border into the tribal areas of Pakistan. He was too old to run the day-to-day operation, so his son Siraj Haqqani took over. The Haqqanis were originally from Khowst Province, but had settled in North Waziristan in Pakistan. They ran a network of Taliban resistance fighters, suicide bombers more closely affiliated with Al Qaida, and narco-trafficking networks from their headquarters near Miram Shah, North Waziristan. They were also a high value target to everyone in the US SOF community. In short, if 524 wanted a meeting to talk about the Haqqanis, Pluto wanted Joe to make that meeting and find out why.

524 triggered the meeting with Joe using a standard call-in "parole"

to Joe's base of operations in Jalalabad. 524 had a non-attributable mobile phone and the Jalalabad base had a bank of equally non-attributable mobile phones that were used by Adam and Joe's agents to call in and trigger meetings. Joe had a set of questions he needed to pose to 524 at this meeting, but first he had to find out why 524 scheduled the meeting at all. So, Joe was driving around the back streets of Tor Kham, on a very cold March night, doing his best to avoid entering into Pakistan, avoiding the ten-ton smuggling trucks running without lights heading into and out of Pakistan while keeping in radio contact with the security team following him in one of the ubiquitous Toyota Hi-Lux pickup trucks.

Joe was about to make the final turn into the meeting location when an explosion to his left hit the Pajero full on and tipped the vehicle on its right side. The explosion had collapsed the wall of the mud brick building into the street and buried the Pajero frame with rubble. After the fact, Joe realized this was a good thing because the rubble served as a wall against the Kalashnikov bullets aimed at his truck. Behind Joe, the Hi-Lux stopped and three of the four passengers were out on the street returning fire with M4 carbines and a M242 Squad Automatic Weapon known simply as a SAW. The driver of the truck maneuvered the armored Hi-Lux so it could provide some cover to the SOF fighters and their effort to extricate Joe from the Pajero. The ambushers were at a disadvantage because the security team had the latest version of SOF night vision googles, green eyes in SOF parlance, and their weapons had both flash and sound suppressors. That meant they could see the ambushers without being pinpointed.

The voices on the radio were calm and relatively quiet; the team headsets kept the noise of the gunfire at bay.

"*3, you got the guy on the roof?*"

"*Roger,*" a pause and a burst of four rounds from the SAW, "*target down.*"

"*2, you got the guy at 12 o'clock.*"

Another muffled round, "*6, did you really need to ask?*"

"*1, can you get to 5 and see what we need? We need to get off the X as soon as possible.*"

The Ranger driving the truck climbed out of the Hi-Lux with a small crowbar in his left hand and his suppressed 1911A1 automatic in his right hand He had to get into the Pajero by way of the rear hatch since the right side of the truck was now face down on the street and the left side was exposed to the ambushers. He holstered the pistol, used a two-handed grip on the crowbar to pop the double locked hatch, and forced his way into the truck. As he climbed in, he turned on the red filtered high powered light attached to his helmet. The inside of the small truck was filled with a beam of red light focused wherever he looked. This made anything red look black in the beam of light. He could see there was plenty of black liquid in the truck.

Joe turned his head and looked at his rescuer, "Will you cut me free from the seatbelt. I definitely want to get outta here." There were Kalashnikov rounds hitting the front of the truck and the windshield. None of the rounds penetrated the armor, but each round that hit the windshield turned another part of the screen into a spiderweb. Joe's face was streaked with blood, but head wounds always bleed like crazy, so the Ranger knew that was not of concern. The shoulder wound from crashing into the right side of the truck looked serious but not life threatening. One or the other of the wounds were the most likely source of the black streaks along the entire right side of the truck. The Ranger used a belt cutting knife he had pulled from a Velcro pocket on his armored vest to start the process of getting Joe out of his seat.

"Good thing the Pajero came from Pakistan, eh?" The Ranger's face was partly obscured by the helmet, clear ballistic glasses and boom mike, but he definitely had a smile. Joe realized that the fact that he was driving a right-hand drive vehicle in a left-hand drive country had just saved his life. On the left side of the truck, he would have faced the full concussive force of the improvised explosive device. He also realized that if the Ranger was smiling, he was probably not in as much danger as his body told him he was.

"Never underestimate the value of an inconvenience," Joe said as the Ranger finished the final cuts to get him out of the shoulder and waist belt.

"No need to shout."

"What?" Joe was not wearing the headsets that his security team was wearing and his left ear had taken the full concussion from the blast. His right ear was still plugged with the earbud, so he couldn't hear much but ringing. The driver waved an index finger and just got to work dropping Joe's seat back into the rear compartment so he could pull him out of the Pajero and back to the Hi-Lux. He keyed his microphone to the net.

"6, we got a live one here. I'm pulling him out. What do you want to do with the Pajero?"

"1, Just put a thermite in the cab once you are clear and we will get the hell out of here."

The Ranger pulled Joe out of the truck and helped him into the bed of the pickup so that he didn't have to move too many joints that might be seriously damaged from blast injuries. He wrapped an armored blanket around Joe, carefully placed a neck brace , slipped a spare helmet on his head, and said, "Don't move, I'll be right back." He then ran back to the Pajero, pulled the pin on the thermite grenade and called to his partners, *"All, switch off the green eyes, Thermite going into the Pajero."*

As soon as he heard the confirmation, the driver released the spoon on the grenade and tossed it onto the driver's seat of the Pajero. Three seconds later, the thermite ignited and turned the truck into a single torch of white light. It would be a minute or two before the fire chewed through the firewall of the truck and another minute before the diesel fuel ignited adding to the fire. Nothing would be left of the Pajero except melted armor. They had about three minutes to clear out.

By the time he was back in the truck, his teammates were already on board. The team leader, *"Red6,"* was already in the bed of the truck working on their wounded Klingon. The Toyota backed up, did a relatively slow K-turn in the street and headed back to Jalalabad.

"Red6 to Mike6, we are RTB with our wounded Klingon. RTB, I say again, RTB." Silence. The truck was already on one of the main highways and accelerating out of Tor Kham. The Ranger driver was doing his best to avoid swerving around parked and slow-moving vehicles, but

it was still grim in the back and the team leader multi-tasked doing triage on Joe and communicating to the rest of the SOF elements involved in the operation.

"Any Mike station, this is Red6. DO YOU READ ME." The Ranger team leader was worried that the concussion from the blast had damaged the antenna on their Hi-Lux. He needed to switch over to the command net to arrange a MEDEVAC at an LZ on the Tor Kham to Jalalabad road. If the radio antenna was done, it meant stopping the truck, setting up a satcom rig and calling in that way. Not hard, but it would take time and he wasn't entirely sure how much time Joe had before he would go into shock.

"Red6, Mike 3. We read you. We are working toward our RV location with Mike6. We are not in contact with him at this point. Will advise."

"Red 6, roger. Out." Radio contact was notoriously bad in Eastern Nangarhar. There was a debate inside SOF whether it was the walled compounds reinforced with rebar making each house a small Faraday cage, or if it was Pakistan army efforts to jam all radio traffic around the border. No one knew, but the Ranger team leader couldn't worry about the MIKEs right now. He had to switch to the command net, call in the MEDEVAC, stabilize his patient and be prepared to fight if need be as they headed to a pre-established LZ where a SOF Blackhawk could take their Klingon to the field hospital in Bagram.

The three-car MIKE team worked their way to the rendezvous or RV location on the outskirts of Tor Kham. Their boss, CW5 Bill Jameson, call sign Mike6, was prepositioned in a non-descript Toyota sedan, managing the entry and exit route from his car. Given the fact that there had been little to see or do but observe and report on their Klingon's progress into the city, comms had been little more than 30 minute radio checks. They were coming up on time for another 30 minute check when the they converged on Jameson's vehicle. The tires were flattened, the vehicle was tipped on its left side and someone had used a heavy duty pry bar to open the driver's door.

Bill Jameson was missing.

Sue spent the day working out the logistics of getting to Italy and did a little one-on-one computer coordination with Ginger to make sure he was good with her plans for turnovers once he had escaped Iraqi Kurdistan. It was a busy day, but by the time she was finished, she was confident that she had a reasonable backwards planning sequence for the move and a straightforward method for getting the various jobs done. She crawled into her cot inside the shipping container that she called home with a degree of satisfaction.

Sue's computer made an annoying sound when it received a message from 171. Somewhere between a cat howl and fingernails on a chalkboard. The 171 technical support officer Marconi warned her that she wouldn't like it, but she definitely couldn't sleep through it. Sue sat up in her bunk and looked at the laptop and wondered what would be the consequences inside the container if she just fired a single 9mm round into the laptop. Eventually, she just decided to make the laptop quit by answering the mail.

It was an email from Massoni. "Sue, hook up a SVTC, now." Sue was immediately full awake. Massoni was never that blunt or that directive and he rarely used her first name in email traffic. She turned on the lights in the container, started a cup of coffee, used a wet one to wash the sleep out of her face and started setting up for a SVTC. She looked at her men's dive watch on a nylon watchband. Big face, big hands, easy to see day or night even when you have only had a couple of hours sleep. Sue said to herself, "2220hrs at Bragg. This can't be good news."

When the screen finally showed Massoni, his face filled the screen and Sue thought it looked like he might actually be crying. Short of the end of the world, Sue couldn't imagine what would make Jim Massoni cry. In any event, it was clearly a call that needed to start more formally than their regular banter.

"Sergeant Major, what is going on?"

Massoni took a deep breath, or perhaps sighed, and said, "Sue, there has been an incident on the Pak-Afghan border. It was an ambush using one of our assets as bait to bring in a 171 case officer."

Sue swallowed hard. Sometimes, it almost seemed if you didn't ask, the bad news wouldn't arrive. After a few seconds, she gave up and said, "Jim, who is our man there?"

"Adam and Joe are out there. Joe was the target. His vehicle was blasted to hell and gone by an IED. He is in the hospital at Bagram. Head wounds, concussion, broken ribs and shoulder, dislocated knee. He is stable," Massoni paused. "Sue, they knew about the MIKE coverage. And...," Massoni swallowed hard, "they kidnapped Bill Jameson."

Sue felt the blood rush out of her head; nauseous, she had to turn away from the screen. She pushed the laptop away, it fell on the floor as she turned away and faced the end of her shipping container. Bill Jameson. Her boss for years. The founder of "the MIKEs." Over twenty years in the Special Operations Forces including ten as a SOF raid team member, five as a squadron raid team leader, and another eight as the first team leader for Surveillance and Reconnaissance (S&R) Squadron. As Sue's memories flooded with emotions, she heard the computer generated voice of Massoni.

"Sue, look at me. Come back to the screen, Sue."

She put the laptop back on the small computer desk and said, "Jim, what's going on?"

"We don't know much. There is a full Ranger company working the two sites. The second S&R team, QUEBEC team, just flew into country and they are conducting a full search of both sites to find out anything that was left behind. The MIKEs have been sent back to the SOF compound in J-Bad. They didn't like it, but there is no way they could do the needful today."

Massoni moved his head so that his entire face filled the screen,

"Jed has decided to delay the move to Italy. He is assembling a 171 team to go out to Bagram and then throw everything we have at the targets to find Bill. He feels that the only way we are going to find Bill is to gather as much intelligence as we can as fast as we can." Massoni paused and then said, "Jed wants to know two things: First, will your ops schedule allow you to come with us and spend at least two weeks in Afghanistan and second, can you keep focused? We both know you are very close to Bill. The only way we are going to save Bill is if everyone is at the top of their game. I told him yes and yes, but he wanted me to hear it from you."

Sue was the one crying now. Not sobbing, not sniveling, but quietly crying. She knew that a captured member of the armed forces had little chance of surviving even the first few hours of a capture much less day. The extremists were currently all about video executions. Still, if anyone could find Bill, it was the SOF units in Afghanistan and if it was going to be a SOF unit in Afghanistan, Sue was determined she was going to be in that unit. She wiped her face and nose and looked directly into the camera, "Jim, I'm in. Nothing could prevent me from being in."

"OK, that's settled. We are flying into Aviano in the SOF commander's G5 aircraft. Wheels up here at 0800Z which means we should be in Aviano at 15Z. You need to be in Aviano RFN. Catch whatever you can to meet us. Check?"

RFN. Under stress, Massoni reverted to Ranger First Sergeant speak. RFN meant Right Fucking Now. Sue looked at her watch. Cyprus was GMT or Zulu time plus 2. She had twelve hours to get to Aviano. Earlier would be better. RFN would be best. She responded, "Jim, I will be there. I will whistle up the MILATT bird and get to Aviano in advance of your bird. Aviano is the refueling stop, right?"

"Check, Sue. We can get around 4500 miles in the Commander's GULFSTREAM 5 before she needs to drink. At Mach .85, it is the quickest way we can get to Bagram. Pack for winter combat. Roger?"

"I need either an M4 or a MP5 from the 171 armory. Otherwise I'm set. I'm packing now. Every minute counts."

"Roger, Sue. We are bringing Flash and Pluto to brief us in flight so we should have full SA before we land. Pigpen is the only other collector we could get free right now. He is flying in from Djibouti to Aviano. It is going to be just six of us to get the job done. Out here." The screen went blank.

Sue didn't know what to think. Bill saved her life in Jalalabad, she had to repay the favor. But there were plenty of different enemy forces in Eastern Afghanistan. Which one had Bill? And where? Until she knew more, there was nothing she could do but make a packing list, pack to the list, wake up the MILATT and get to Aviano. No sense in working the problem until she knew something. One thing she did not have to check was her ops schedule. Since she had expected to spend at least two weeks in Aviano, she had no meetings scheduled for the rest of the month. Sue knew that if they didn't find Bill in less than two weeks, they wouldn't find him alive.

Once she was done with the list, Sue had an hour to sit still and think. Sitting still had never been one of her strong points and that had been a challenge when she transitioned from her time as a military intelligence warrant officer to a member of a team on SOF Surveillance and Reconnaissance. There were more than a few shrinks working at SOF and at OGA who pushed Sue to admit that she lost her leg because she was too impatient. Over time, she had found the only way to manage her restlessness and her impatience was turn on her iPod, plug in her Bose headphones and listen to either Bach or Mozart. The complexity of these two composers helped take her mind off all the nagging, peripheral noise inside her head. Bach was the choice for these early morning hours. As Bach started to calm her frayed nerves, Sue remembered scenes from her first days in S&R and how Jameson had served as a mentor and surrogate father along the way.

She remembered…

Within a few days of her graduation from the S&R selection course and after she had in-processed at S&R Squadron headquarters at Ft. Bragg, she was called to the office of her new team boss, Bill Jameson. Sue had already used her Ft. Bragg network to determine what sort of team leader Jameson might be. His background was relatively standard for SOF. First tour at the 82nd Airborne, followed by Special Forces. Jameson worked his way up to team sergeant in 10th Special Forces based in Bad Tolz, Germany. After that, Sue's network intelligence became a little vague.

Some said that Jameson went to the warrant officer course planning to stay in Special Forces; others said he left SF as an NCO, attended SOF selection to be a member of the counterterrorism raid teams in SOF and was promoted inside "the unit" to warrant officer. Either way, the story ended with him leaving the raid teams and serving as one of the founders of S&R. He attended the training course in Hereford with the UK Special Reconnaissance Regiment to understand how the best military surveillance team in the world trained. Then he began building a program at Ft. Bragg. Before the S&R squadron was fully established, they were already "downrange" hunting war criminals in the Balkans. No matter what else she heard, Sue realized she was checking into a unit run by a SOF legend.

Jameson's office was a small room at the end of the team bay, painted years ago in an Army pale green. Jameson was sitting behind a metal, army issue desk that was also pale green. He was wearing a faded set of olive drab green jungle fatigues known as OG107s. Totally sterile with no nametags, unit patches or badges. Standing next to him was Command Sergeant Major Jim Massoni. Massoni was a recently promoted sergeant major and an arrival from the Ranger Regiment. He was still wearing his high and tight haircut and an apparent hard-edged demeanor. He was also in sterile OG107s but Sue noticed Massoni's well-worn jungle boots were still spit shined to a high gloss at the toes. Sue felt out of place in her standard European camouflage pattern Battle Dress Uniform and jump boots with her red beret rolled into the cargo pocket on the left side of her trousers.

Behind the two team leaders were three satellite maps. One was a city map of Belgrade, Serbia, the second a city map of Nairobi, Kenya and the third was a city map of Qandahar, Afghanistan. Sue was not surprised at either of the first two maps. Belgrade was an important site in the SOF mission to find and capture Balkan war criminals, known in the community as "persons indicted for war crimes" or compressed to PIFWCs. The Nairobi map was likely based on the East Africa embassy bombings by Al Qaida. Qandahar was not on her register as someplace that SOF would work.

Jameson focused her attention quickly. So quickly, she forgot to ask about Qandahar. "O'Connell, congratulations on graduating from selection and welcome to the team. I have looked at your file both before and during selection and you have the background to suc-ceed."

Sue thought, here it comes, the implied "for a girl."

Instead, Jameson continued, "But you need to know that selection didn't teach you shit about what we do. It only gave me the approval to give you a chance to learn what we do."

Massoni added at this point, "Chief, we don't have time for train-ing, so we expect you to learn on the job. Check?"

Sue wasn't entirely certain how the team worked, but she knew how to respond when a Sergeant Major spoke. Sure, she was a Warrant Officer and theoretically outranked a Sergeant Major, but everyone in the Army knew that no one outranked a Sergeant Major. "Check, Sergeant Major."

Jameson reentered the discussion, "O'Connell, we are a close-knit team and you are replacing one of the founders of S&R. Sandy Mikelson just got promoted to Sergeant Major and he is leaving for the Sergeant Major's Academy and then for a job as the Command Sergeant Major on one of our SOF raid squadrons. It means you are taking the place of a guy who helped design what we do. Don't expect to fit in right away or to have anyone on the team expect you to know how to do stuff. The team won't be thrilled to have a female on the team, but just between us, Jim and I asked for you. That request was not only because you demonstrated excellent capability in selection, but also because you are a female operator. We have targets in a dozen different countries right now and in most of those countries a team of young, fit men is not good enough. That doesn't mean you will be asked to do anything different from the rest of the team, just that your profile in country is going to change our image a bit and make it easier to hunt the assholes we hunt."

Jameson paused, took a sip from a white ceramic coffee mug with master parachute wings embossed on the side. He ended the in-brief simply by saying, "Just follow instructions, pay attention to anything you hear and see, and execute the requirement as given. Oh, and one more thing, don't spend a lot of time worrying about what the Sergeant Major thinks, he doesn't know shit either."

"Boss, that is so cruel. I've been here ninety days and made one rotation. I know enough to know I don't know shit. You don't have to rub it in." Massoni turned to Sue, "I have to put up with this sort of treatment all the time here just because I just came from the Ranger Regiment and most of these guys come from Special Forces. They think we are all knuckle draggers at the Regiment even if many of us started in Special Forces and, perhaps, even put them through the SF Qualification course." Massoni turned to Jameson with a knowing look.

Jameson responded, "You look at your knuckles recently, Jim?"

Massoni made a face like he was hurt and turned to Sue, "See what I mean?"

Sue left the office and headed to the team bay where the S&R kept the various tools of their trade, their vehicles, bunks and a small gym. She wasn't sure how it would work out with the team, but she was pleased so far with the team management.

Jameson couldn't believe he had been so stupid. After years in the field, he had let his guard down and now he was in the back of a Toyota Land Cruiser with a hood on his head, ropes on his ankles and wrists and headed to God knows where. The surveillance serial plan had been sufficiently mundane that he had decided to give part of the team a break. He would run the serial from a car rather than his normal position in the back of the "Magic Bus" where he had multiple radios, cell phone intercept capability and a large map board so he could track the team while someone else did the driving. This was supposed to be a basic "in and out" counter-surveillance job where his team would stakeout the route and let the Klingon and his security detachment do the rest.

Jameson's stakeout position had been on the west side of Tor Kham in an abandoned industrial area that looked like the set for a post-apocalypse movie. The metal-sided buildings were partially collapsed, the wire fences that identified specific properties were lying on the ground and dogs ran wild throughout the area. Through the windshield he could see small fires burning where homeless families were living on the edge of the city. He was sitting in the beat-up Corolla listening to the team comms and the communications between the team and the security detachment when he saw the barrel of an AK47 pressed against his window. How the Afghan had made it up to the car without him noticing was still a mystery, but he attributed part of the problem to the fact that he hadn't had any sleep for a day and a half. He regularly lectured the team on the risk of "micro-sleep" where a tired operator loses consciousness for a few seconds as his brain demands rest. Micro-sleep was the cause of more than one vehicle accident both in warzones and back in CONUS and it would appear he had fallen prey to the same problem with even more dire consequences.

After an hour of personal recrimination as he bumped around the back of the truck, Jameson managed to focus his attention on his present condition and potential future scenarios. Here were the facts as he saw them:

He was alive and that meant they intended to keep him alive for some period of time for a purpose he couldn't determine;

He was in a vehicle on dirt roads. His backache told him that much.

If he intended to live, he needed to escape. SOF would attempt a rescue, but by then, he could be dead.

His kidnappers were not the most careful of villains. While his hands and feet were tied and then tied together by a length of rope between them, they were both secured in front of him rather than in a much more painful and secure pose behind his back. That meant he could touch his legs with his hands. He reached down carefully to his boots and activated the GPS signaling device in the heel of his right boot. It would send out a satellite signal as long as the lithium batteries held out and so long as they allowed him to keep his boots. It wasn't much, but when Jameson completed that small, clandestine act, he felt better. Each little victory was good for his morale as well as good at keeping his mind off the eventual consequences of his capture.

T he flight out of Aviano would have been good duty if the reason for their travel wasn't so grim. Sue had travelled military aircraft for most of her career. Military aircraft were designed for cargo with roller conveyor systems down the middle of the aircraft and red nylon sling seats along the interior skin of the aircraft. Most MILAIR flights were a mix with passengers crammed into shoulder-to-shoulder into sling seats facing 8 foot by 8 foot cargo pallets. MILAIR was noisy, either too cold or too hot and definitely not a good ride for someone with a below the knee prosthetic. Instead on this flight, she was flying in the Commander's G5 which was the same size as trophy jets flown by rock stars and millionaires. It was configured with more seats and where the couches were usually placed there was a work table near the rear cargo door. Still, it was a long distance from the "normal" routine.

Pluto and Flash worked together to build a briefing for the entire 171 team as they crossed the Aegean and headed over the Black Sea. Jed Smith, the 171 commander, sat with his deputy, Jim Massoni, at the front of the cabin. This was not the first time and probably wouldn't be the last time that either man had been on a search and rescue mission that they knew could change at any minute into a search and recovery mission. After a brief discussion, they put on their "command faces" and walked down the aisle to Sue and Pigpen encouraging both to get some sleep before they settled into their own seats next to the work table and tried to follow their own orders. They pointed out that there would be no time to sleep for the early days on the ground in Afghanistan. Jim said to the two 171 operators,

70

"We will wake up in about three hours before touchdown for a team briefing by the brain trust. Don't overthink this now 'cause you don't know shit."

Sue looked out the window and down at the cirrus clouds that were screaming across the winter sky in what was either Turkey or Azerbaijan, she wasn't sure. She put on her Bose headphones and turned on Mozart from her iPhone. In 1999, Sue had found a new family on Jameson's team and inside the SOF community. It was a family because Jameson knew how to keep the team focused on the mission and on keeping each other safe. Team members were expected to participate in the entire operational planning phase as well as the execution phase. Jameson ran a team meeting in a way that she hadn't seen before in the Army. After the basic mission brief, Jameson would ask each member of the team for comments. Usually, an Army leader would ask "Any comments or questions?" which translated into "we're done here unless you want to drag this briefing out." When Jameson asked your thoughts, he expected you to say something. It took longer, but the result was the planning phase was just that much better.

After Sue returned from her father's funeral and back to work in Afghanistan, Jameson designed a surveillance serial so that he would spend some time with Sue "two up" in one of the vehicles. Sue was in the back of a taxi in an Afghan burqa that smelled like goat and Jameson was in the front wearing local kit that told anyone who could see in the car that he was the driver for a wealthy Afghan. He used the time to quiz Sue on her family, how she was handling the unexpected loss of a parent, and how she felt about returning to the mission so quickly. It was a mix of pep talk, counseling, and evaluation, but Jameson carried the discussion in a way that Sue never felt that she was being interrogated. That night, Sue realized how much she thought of Jameson as a surrogate father or, more accurately, a favorite uncle. She also realized how much work Jameson did to make each member of the team feel the same way.

After losing her leg in the gunfight in Jalalabad, Sue had learned it was Jameson who made it to her and kept her from going into shock. He and Massoni visited Sue at Walter Reed and kept in touch via email all through the Farm. Sue hadn't had a boyfriend since arriving in S&R. Too many tdys, too little time back in CONUS, and a strict code of "no fraternization" inside the Squadron. Bill and Max Creeter were the closest she had to surrogate fathers after her real father died. Now, her father, her grandfather and Max were all buried. Her father was killed working as a double agent against the Russians. Her grandfather was killed by the Russian mafia and Max Creeter was killed protecting her mother from the same crew. Jameson was the one stable male force in her life She was not going to lose another member of the family.

She couldn't imagine how she was going to sleep, but eventually, sleep took her away from her troubles and passed her off to "the dream." Sue was in an unfamiliar warzone. She could hear the voices of team members calling for her help. As she looked around the smoke of the battlefield, she saw different faces: her father, Max Creeter and Bill Jameson all calling for help. Sue was on her back in a foxhole and tried to run to help them. Then she realized she couldn't find her prosthetic. She tried to hop on her right leg to get to the first victim pleading for her help – her father – and she kept falling down until he disappeared. The same thing happened as she approached Max. Finally, she started to approach Jameson and Sue could see the prosthetic just a short reach away and then it disappeared.

She woke soaked in sweat. Luckily before they left Aviano, she had switched out of her uniform and into a set of Under Armor sweats with the SOF logo on the chest. A spearhead inside an oval topped by an airborne tab. Nearly same logo her grandfather might have worn, unofficially of course, on his field uniform when he was in the OSS. They had dimmed the cabin lights to give the team a chance to sleep. Sue looked at the luminescent hands of her watch. It was 1900Z. She had been asleep for 3 hours. She did the quick calculation in her head. They left at 1600Z. It was nearly six hours to Bagram. It was time to get up. Sue headed to the pair of lavatories in the rear of the aircraft. She passed the "brain trust" table now occupied by 171 commander Jed Smith, Massoni, and the 171 analysts only known among the team as Pluto and Flash. Sue knew Flash's last name only because she saw her once before in a military uniform when they were briefing the SOF commander. Billings was what the name tape had said then. Now she was in desert camouflage trousers and her standard black t-shirt. Well, Flash would stay just Flash as far as she was concerned.

Massoni looked up from his coffee cup. It was a stainless steel mug with command sergeant major stripes etched on one side and Yes, I do hate you on the other. "Good morning, sunshine. Time to get to work. You do what you need to do in the port lavatory. Pigpen is doing whatever he does to make himself beautiful in the starboard side. Don't worry, you are only about five minutes behind him." Sue didn't know why, but the return of Massoni the joker seemed like good news. When she returned from the lavatory, dressed in Desert Camouflage trousers, a tan long sleeved t-shirt, and her specially fitted desert boots, she joined the table and received coffee from Massoni's flask.

"The CG has a coffee maker in the galley in the front, but it makes crap coffee. You need Sergeant Major coffee."

"Thanks, Jim. I definitely need it right now."

Smith was opposite Sue at the table and started the briefing. "So, while we were all sleeping, Pluto and Flash were working and, it looks like they were very successful. No reason to be super optimistic…yet, but I do feel better about the mission than I have for the last 12 hours. Pluto, it's your briefing. Do it."

Pluto got his nickname from his enormous ears that looked even larger given the bone thin, shaved head where they were attached. He looked about 19 but was more likely fifteen years older given his background and his rank. He was wearing a full Army Battle Dress Uniform with his name, Jackson, and his rank, Sergeant First Class. Sue hadn't worked with Pluto in the past and this was the first time she had seen him in uniform and the first time she had seen his last name. He was the AFPAK analyst for 171. Flash, the Hizballah and Eastern Med Sunni extremist analyst, had been her partner while in Cyprus. What Sue had noticed during her in-processing at 171 was that Pluto always spoke just above a whisper so you needed to pay attention if you intended to get anything out of his briefing.

"Sir, here's what we know. We have received both SIGINT and

an imagery feed from an OGA UAV that was running the border. As soon as the ambush occurred, they focused their collection on the entire area. It turns out that the UAV operators were on their toes and realized that there were two different attacks taking place. This particular UAV had a pair of cameras, usually used to give better depth perception in targeting. In this case, they focused one camera on Joe and one on Chief Jameson. They saw the kidnapping and then used the bird to follow the kidnappers. The signals feed was from a pair of cellphones on the Pakistan network that bleeds over into Afghanistan. The Pashtu language gurus at Kabul Station have translated the take for us. It seems the ambush on Joe wasn't linked at all to the kidnap of Chief Jameson. The kidnappers aren't part of the Haqqani network. They talk like they are just tribal villains."

As Pluto paused to drink some coffee and rub his face, Sue realized that neither Pluto nor Flash had slept in in the past 24 to 36 hours since they probably did a full work day yesterday before being pulled back to the warehouse on an emergency call. Pluto continued, "The UAV tracked them to a village about 10km inside Pakistan in the Mohmand Tribal Agency. The UAV is in orbit and as of an hour ago, one of our birds was launched to take over the watch."

In 2003 when Sue was last in Afghanistan, the only UAVs in the area were the OGA birds. SOF needed their own and did a crash buy of multiple birds that they could use in any combat theatre. Some were pure surveillance, some were armed. It would appear that the SOF UAV plan was now operational and the airspace was shared by both Kabul station, that "other government agency" as SOF called the CIA and SOF command in Bagram.

Flash took over the briefing and started by showing two faces on her laptop. "According to the SOF and OGA records, these are the two tribal leaders who are competing for power in the area. Din Mohammed and Abdul Khan. Both are Mohmand tribesmen and they are cousins." Flash put on her most academic face. "The Pashtu tribal world is known by academics as a segmentary lineage system. It means everyone is related in some way to a mythical ancestor and land is distributed down a single line in a family. If you are in the line, you win. If you are not, you lose. If your cousin wins, then you hate your cousin more than anyone else on the planet. Perfect, eh?"

Smith interjected, "Flash, thanks for that, but how does it help us? Do we know which of these two guys have Bill? Do we have any leverage on either of them?"

"Boss, the only real answer at this point is I don't know. What I do know is Din Mohammed has made a career as a kidnapper. He regularly grabs Pakistan government officials and holds them hostage until he gets something. Usually money, but sometimes a clinic or a water well. If he is our kidnapper, it means that he doesn't intend to kill Chief Jameson, he intends to sell him to the highest bidder. It means we have some time. Abdul Khan is a more radicalized tribal and a member of the Tehrik-e-Taliban, the Pakistan Taliban. They are marginally allied with the Taliban on the Afghan side of the border. We don't know if he has any links to Al Qaida or any of the other Sunni extremists in Pakistan like the Lashkar-e-Taiba. If he has the Chief, he may be interested in a trade for some relative or another TTP leader currently being held by the Pakistan Army. Or..."

Smith raised and eyebrow and waved his hand, "Out with it."

"Or, it may be part of a larger effort by extremists affiliated with the Haqqani network who have ties with the Pakistan intelligence service known as the Inter-Services Intelligence Directorate or ISID. The Haqqanis and their Al Qaida pals are big on killing hostages. That is the most dangerous possibility and it means we need to get the Chief out of harm's way RFN."

"So, good, bad and ugly." Massoni was never one for long briefings.

Smith nodded and said, "Jim, you got it. We don't have any feed that really helps. With Joe in the hospital, we need to focus on setting up meetings with any contacts that Joe or Adam have on the border and squeeze what we can out of them. Adam has already set up emergency meetings with his sources and sent us contact information for Joe's guys. O'Connell, you and Taylor will do the needful on that front. We did receive notice that when we touch down at Bagram, there will be a reception committee including Deputy Commander, SOF and some goober from OGA, I'm assuming the station, though they do have a presence in Bagram." Sue knew Pigpen's last name was Taylor, but she had never heard it spoken by anyone except Smith. Just the use of his last name reminded her that this was serious business.

Smith turned to Pigpen and Sue. "You got anything to add?"

Sue asked, "Do we know if Bill had a GPS tracker on him? We used to carry two. One in our load bearing vests and one embedded in a boot heel. I don't know if that is still the case."

Flash shook her head. "I know they checked for the GPS in the LBV. Is the heel one

on the same frequency?"

"It wasn't a couple of years ago, but I don't know now." Massoni finally had something to say.

Pigpen looked up from his coffee. "Are we going to get clearance to cross the Durand Line? When I was here with SOF raiders in 2002, the border between Pakistan and Afghanistan was considered a hard-line you didn't cross."

Smith looked at Pigpen and said, "Taylor, if we have to go to China to recover Chief Jameson, we are going to go. That is more or less what Commander, SOF told me before we left."

"Check, boss. I just wanted to know if we were going to pursue or if we were going to have to lure the creeps across the border."

"The answer is whatever it takes." Smith looked at his watch. "OK, get your kit packed up and get your uniforms on. Bagram is an Air Force base and we can expect the normal conventional force protocol. No need to ruffle feathers at this point." Smith stood up and headed for the port lavatory. Pluto headed for the starboard one.

Flash looked up and said, "Well, I guess we know the difference between men and women's bladders."

Massoni snarled, "Or maybe between officers and enlisted?"

Sue said, "Or the boss knows rule number one – always pee when you can." She turned toward her seat in the forward part of the aircraft.

BISHOP IN JEOPARDY

They stepped off the aircraft late at night, under bright lights that turned the runway apron silvery white with no shadows. Even at this hour, aircraft, vehicles and men moved across the tarmac. A USAF base in a warzone is always working. Snow was falling and Sue was shocked by the cold, despite multiple layers on including long underwear under her uniform and a sweater, a light-weight down parka and her military Gore-tex with gloves and a tan watch cap. It was March and it was still winter here in Afghanistan. It would probably be worse in the mountains on the border.

Sue stepped off the aircraft, with Pluto and Flash behind her. Smith and Massoni and Pigpen were already on the ground. Jed Smith was shaking hands with the Deputy Commander of SOF. Because SOF had two major missions in the Global War on Terror - in Afghanistan and in Iraq - the command had to split forces and run two command structures. Commander, SOF spent most of his time in Balad, Iraq. The other deputy was based full time in Bagram. The links between Ft. Bragg, Balad and Bagram were tight with the daily briefing among the three seniors at 1200hrs Zulu. They were in regular, informal contact as well. The Deputy in Bagram was a senior Naval Special Warfare officer who spoke Persian and had served multiple tours in Afghanistan starting in 2002. Why SEALS were serving in Afghanistan, a land-locked country, was anyone's guess, but that was well above Sue's pay grade. It was clear from their body language that Smith knew DC/SOF well and they were already deep in conversation. That meant Sue had a chance to get closer to the discussion between Massoni and the bear.

In the surreal light, Sue saw an even more surreal image to her right. It appeared that Massoni was hugging a bear. By this time, Flash was on the ground standing to Sue's right. "Who's the bear? Or, should I say, who's bear is it? I've never been to Afghanistan, do we work with bears?"

"Beats me, but Massoni was just hugging him."

"I guess Massoni trained him."

The bear spoke. "Hey Sue and Flash, what are you doing working for this criminal?"

Massoni turned to face Sue, Flash and now Pluto who was standing to Sue's left. "Pay no attention to Jamie. He's always been a jerk."

"Even when I dragged your sorry ass through Ranger School?"

"Only after I violated my standards and passed you in SF Q course."

As they walked closer, Sue could see Jamie's face surrounded by a well-worn Russian fur hat. The last time she had seen Jamie was in Baghdad when they were the target of a very large IED that turned Jamie's armored vehicle into a slab of melted steel and fiberglass. Now he was wearing some sort of sheepskin coat that might have been white originally but was now a dull brown. It extended from his shoulders to his ankles. He was wearing fur boots which completed his fur ensemble. Sue would have described him to her mom as "an axe handle wide and about as hard as granite." Given his current attire, it was no wonder she thought he was a bear.

Flash recovered first and said to Jamie, "Klingon, how's the ear?" The last time she had seen Jamie, he had stitches holding his ear on his head and a cast on his arm. Flash had "nursed" him back to health, or so she told Sue.

"Flash, good to see you though I thought you didn't like the cold."

"Give me a hug, Jamie and I'll be fine."

"Hey, Jamie, don't go fraternizing with my troops." It was not clear if Massoni was serious.

"OK, Jim. I will stick to business right now. I have two Mi17s waiting over here to take you to your new home in the Konar. It is very scenic, along the Pech River. For you non-linguists here, Pech means twisty or screwy. So, we are going to be living on the Screwy River, at least until we ruck up and head to the border. You got your stuff ready to go? I will have my guys do the cross load and we will pull pitch and go."

Smith walked over to the crew. "Mr…?"

Massoni took the lead, "Boss, this bearlike creature is Jamie Shenk. Back in the age of steam, he was another one of my students at Pineland University and then was my Ranger buddy in Ranger School. He left SF after 25 and went over to the dark side. He is an OGA officer now, running a detachment of Afghan commandos based south of Asadabad on the border with Mohmand Agency. He is reliable though I wouldn't trust him not to steal our kit."

"So cruel, Jim."

"So true, Jamie."

Smith held out his hand, "Good to meet you. I just talked to my boss over there who said that you're our quickest way in and our best support team for recovering Bill Jameson. You also have the only assets directly in the target area You been read in?"

Jamie nodded and offered a bit of deference to Smith, but only a bit. "Sure, Colonel. I was in the intel shack here when we got the UAV feed. I am familiar with the area and know the Mohmand tribals, who are the likely candidates for the crime. If you are ok with the rest of the story on the birds, I would like to get outta here and into the Konar before dawn. The locals tend to shoot at us when we fly in the daytime."

Jamie continued, "By the way, never fear about the birds. They look old, but these Agency birds have the full glass cockpit that allows NVG flight. Plus, we have two pair of the best Agency pilots on the planet. All you have to do is let my guys load your kit and decide how you want to divide up the team. I have ten gunners with me, so I needed two birds. Station chief said whatever I needed I should take so I'm taking two birds and all the supplies we can carry in them. Just six of you, so split in half and we'll get out of this Air Force version of Hollywood and get into some real bad guy country."

He turned to a series of smaller bear-like characters who were squatting on the tarmac. He spoke to them in Dari and they hopped up and headed for the cargo door of the G5. He turned back and said, "I suspect you have your long guns in the cargo hold. I recommend you recover them now. No telling if we might need them somewhere in flight or when we land. Unpredictable place, the Konar."

Pluto turned to Sue as they walked to the cargo door. He had the hood up on his Gore-Tex parka and looked even more troubled than usual. In his whisper voice, Pluto asked "You trust this guy?"

Flash walked by and said over her shoulder, "Up to a point."

"Up to a point?"

"Up to the point that I don't. Same as I feel about all Klingons."

Sue felt it was time to give Pluto a break from Flash's sarcasm. "First off, he was with me in Baghdad and was nearly killed working a mission for 171. Secondly, I am the daughter and granddaughter of Klingons so I reckon you can trust me and him."

"OK, just asking." Pluto shuffled over to the cargo hatch looking for his long gun case which, courtesy of Massoni, had the Disney image of Pluto attached. Sue found hers with an image of Long John Silver. He had uploaded an MP5 for Sue to use. She was equally good with an M4 or an MP5, but the machine pistol was better for close in work, which Sue expected they would be doing once they got near the captors. She was surprised to see Flash pull out a fiberglass long-gun case with a yellow lightning bolt on the side.

"Flash, what is in the case?"

"Remington M24 rifle, day and night scope, multi-load ammo. I qualified three years ago at SOF sniper school when I was serving in 18th Airborne Corps. They figured it was a throw away slot since I was a girl." Flash smiled, "Ended up I was the best shot in the class. Anyhow, Jed said he might need a long shot before this was over. I'm your chick with the long gun though I really wanted to bring the Barrett."

"Flash, you realize if you had brought the Barrett .50 caliber rifle, you would have to carry it."

"Why do you think I spend so much time in the gym, sweetie?"

"To get men."

"That too." Flash headed to the two Mi17 helicopters which were starting their engines. She walked up to Jamie and asked, "What's with the bear costume?"

"Wait until you get into the Konar, kid. You will want more clothes than you have on now. The local kit is warm and dry and I like to look like a local. It makes it harder for the snipers to decide who to shoot first."

All Flash could do was nod as they approached the noise and aviation fuel smell of the helicopters. Mi17 helicopters are reliable, flying shipping containers. With the proper instrumentation, they can fly anywhere carrying plenty of cargo and men. Not as fast and certainly not as maneuverable as the MH47 or MH60 in the SOF fleet, it was simply a cargo truck with propellers. It was also a ubiquitous cargo truck in Afghanistan flown by the Afghans and multiple members of the International Security Assistance Force. One thing the 171 team learned as soon as they got on board was this was not going to be a flight where they could have any sort of conversation. Mi17s are LOUD.

T he tribal leader walked into the room alone. He was a tall, hawk faced man dressed in a wool shalwar kamiz, the ubiquitous long shirt and pajama pants worn by men, women and children on both sides of the Afghan-Pakistan border. Over the shalwar kamiz, he wore a cream-colored wool vest and a cream-colored wool hat known as a pakol. The first thing that Jameson realized about him was how clean he smelled and how clean his clothes were. This was in direct contrast to Jameson who felt dirty, cold and damp.

The tribal spoke in clear, Pakistani accented English. "You are now my honored guest, Mr. Jameson. We have taken you for a purpose and will treat you well while you are here. My name is Din Mohammed and I am the chief of the Mohmands here on the border. I know you think I am your enemy, but for now, I am not. I am merely a man who holds you temporarily against your will. Eventually, we will trade you for money, or guns, or radios so we can continue our work against the Pakistani government agents who insist they are in charge."

Jameson tried to speak, but all he could get out was a croak because his mouth was so dry. Din Mohammed recognized the sound and turned to the man next to the door. "Chai!" The man came forward with a tray that included a tea pot under an embroidered tea cozy, two opaque, etched glasses, a small number of tea biscuits on a thin china plate, and a small bowl with raisins and walnuts. He pulled a chair over to the bed where Jameson was seated and proceeded to pour out two cups of milky, sweet tea. He waited until Jameson took a sip from the tea cup and then drank from his cup.

"Mr. Jameson, you are important to me. I will profit by trading you. However, I want you to know that my men will kill you if you try to leave this room. We are a simple people and my men do not see any value in making this trade. They speak no English, were not educated in Peshawar as I was, and they are loyal only to me. I fear I will not be able to stop them from doing you harm if you do not obey my instructions. Do you understand?"

Jameson nodded and with some tea down his throat he could speak. He remembered the training from SERE school. The instructors started the class the first day by saying "Survival, Evasion, Resistance, and Escape." That is what you will learn here at our school. Lesson number one: If you are captured, do not give up. You will survive. Lesson number two: Do not be a punk and irritate your captor. You may have to kill him to escape, but in the meantime, be polite and make sure he knows you are a human being just like him. Do what you need to do to survive." Following that instruction, Jameson looked Din Mohammed in the eyes and said, "Thank you for the food and drink. I am humbled by your hospitality." He paused and said, "Are you in contact with my people so that you can get the best possible payment for my safe return?"

Din Mohammed laughed, "My friend, your capture was designed to make a profit. Almost immediately, I was offered twice what I expected for you and, honestly, I took it without question. There will be others who will be disappointed, to include your people who I expected to pay the ransom, but we are honorable men and we always deliver when we agree to a price. I do not know what your friends might pay, but it is a question of my reputation. I hope you understand."

Jameson replied, "Of course. An honorable man must live up to his obligations. I just hope you can at least see to it that you send word to my daughter after I have been taken from here. Just to let her know I was an honorable man to the end."

Din Mohammed bowed his head. "This is something I promise I will do." He turned and left the room and the door closed behind him. Jameson started to eat everything on the tray and drink the tea. He had no idea when or if he would be fed again.

T hey arrived at the forward operating base just at dawn. The Agency pilots had flown through the mountain valleys and into the progressively lighter Eastern sky so Sue and Flash, sitting side by side, were able to see the snowy mountains of "the Konar" during the last half hour of the flight. Sue had flown with the best pilots in the SOF community, the 160th Special Operations Aviation Regiment, in just about every helicopter in the inventory. She was amazed that the Agency pilots were able to carve a route with the same skill as 160th SOAR while flying helicopters that were designed and probably built before Sue entered high school.

Sue looked across the cabin into the faces of Jamie's commandos. Of the five men crowded into the sling seats on the port side of the aircraft, two were sitting with their eyes screwed absolutely shut. The other three were clustered against the port holes on their side of the aircraft speaking some unknown dialect and pointing down at the valley below. Sue had worked with local forces both in the Afghanistan and Iraq, but these men looked to be the toughest she had seen. When she met Jamie in Iraq, she was convinced that his team there looked to be a short step away from a street gang. Here, the commandos were only a short step away from appearing to be the sons of Genghis Khan. They were dressed in a strange blend of traditional wool and leather coupled with black nylon load bearing vests carrying modern firearms. Each of the commandos also carried a two-foot long knife (or perhaps a short sword) which Pluto had told Sue was a traditional "Khyber knife." Pluto told them that most Khyber knives were now made from old truck springs. Strong steel that took a good edge. Pluto closed by describing them simply as "head choppers." Looking at the faces of this unit, Sue was convinced that this was not an exaggeration. Adding to the eccentric nature of their kit, each of Jamie's men carried a very modern, very wicked looking tomahawk.

The two helicopters landed in what probably served in the summer as the soccer pitch of the compound. As they walked off the clamshell rear of the helicopters, Jamie started his description of the compound with a broad sweep of his hand. "Welcome to FOB Pech or FOB Screwy if you prefer. This is a joint OGA and SF base. Currently we have one team from 10th Special Forces, ODA 033." He turned to Massoni and said, "Jim, I doubt any of these youngsters will remember your reputation in Bad Tolz when 10th hung it's beret there, but if we have time, you might want to go over and establish control of the place. I think the ODA commander and his deputy are a bit overwhelmed."

Massoni growled in response, "I would be overwhelmed if I had to live with you."

Jamie ignored Massoni and continued, "So, this place was originally a school in the days of the old King in the 1960s. The commies tried to keep it alive. Eventually, the Konar mujahedin resistance and the rise of the Arab units arriving from Pakistan forced the school to close and it became a Soviet airborne company FOB. Over the last twenty years, it's had plenty of other occupants, but sadly, not a school. My predecessor found the place and used it as a training base to raise this bunch of pirates. After my last tour in Iraq," Jamie looked at Sue, "when she got me blown up…"

Sue intervened at this point and said, "It was not my fault."

"Whatever. Anyhow, the Agency decided to give me a change of scenery. It turns out that my Persian from SF language school worked pretty well here and here I am. We have a full barracks we share with the ODA and a separate one for the commandos, a small arms range so you can zero your weapons, and a full communications package. The SF team is working on what they call village stability operations or VSO. They are training local militias to protect themselves from the extremist creeps who pass through the valley. We do more hostile action hunting the creeps as they come across the border. Speaking of the border, I sent a team into Mohmand territory before I came to pick you up. My partner in crime here at FOB Pech, Wally, is in the TOC and will have an update for sure. Just so you know, I now speak passable military Dari but not much more. Wally is the Dari linguist here. Speaks Pashtu as well. I think he must have a size 10 hat size for all the brains in his knot."

Smith spoke, "I think we need to see the TOC soonest and get Flash and Pluto plugged into both your network and ours."

"Deal, Colonel. Just walk toward the building to our front and enter the red door. No doubt Wally is waiting." Jamie turned to Massoni, Sue and Pigpen. "Follow me with your kit. I will get you settled and then we can regroup at the TOC." Jamie turned to his commandos. Speaking in Dari, he told them where to take the bags and then to bring up the fueling truck to refuel the aircraft. Before Massoni, Sue and Pigpen had finished carrying the team's kit into the building, the aircraft were refueled and had left for some other location on the Afghan side of the border.

Sue had expected the Tactical Operations Center to be a relatively rustic location. Instead, she found the adobe brick exterior disguised a modern interior shell with a half dozen plasma screens and a dozen computer work stations. Pluto and Flash were already using a mix of their own laptops and the OGA computers. Smith and a very tall, very thin balding man who was introduced as Wally were standing in front of a pair of plasma screens with displays of two live UAV feeds. Massoni and Jamie served coffee in porcelain mugs to everyone. Massoni had already let everyone know that Jamie's coffee was "acceptable" but not to Sergeant Major standard.

Jamie said, "This is the advantage of moving into an established FOB. Lots of amenities."

Wally ignored Jamie and started the briefing. "We have tracked the kidnappers to a walled compound just east of the border. They used a smugglers' route from the Konar to Mohmand territory. That was kind of them because we have satellite linked sensors placed on the route. We had the satellite download photos of the truck they used. They are on the display over there," Wally waved over to the far screen, "and we now have two UAVs on station. One armed, one pure sensor bird. The birds will rotate every six hours, but Bagram and station have guaranteed full coverage until we resolve this situation." Sue winced at the use of the term "situation." The "situation" needed to be resolved and Jameson had to be freed.

Wally continued, "The sensor bird has identified two different commo signals from the compound and a weak signal that we think is Jameson's GPS tracker. The commo signals are one cell phone and one satellite phone. Usually a needle in a haystack, but since we had them both identified from Tor Kham, we now have a full lock on the signals and the Fort is providing real time translations." Wally paused to take a drink from the steaming coffee mug. During the pause, Sue took a long look at Wally and realized that just like Pluto and Flash, Wally probably hadn't slept much over the last two days. "Finally, we have six of the Tomahawks moving toward the site to put eyes on the target."

Jamie chimed in. "The Tomahawks are our own little combat force. Some of them were on the bird with us, some are working another AQ target in Asadabad, and the six are on their way into the Mohmand. They are all Hazara Shia tough guys. They hate AQ, the Haqqanis, and any other Islamic extremists who conducted large-scale genocide of their people during the days of the Taliban. The Hazara were the underclass of Afghanistan before the Taliban arrived, "invisible people" who did all the shit work. They are loyal to the cause. And, I promise, they can shoot."

"You said that in Iraq as well." Sue had to break her silence simply so that she felt part of the discussion. Jameson and Smith had both warned Sue that her single greatest flaw was impatience and she was just ready to "ruck up" and save Jameson. Talking through a plan wasn't something Sue liked though she had learned from Jameson early on her first rotation that talking through a plan made for a better plan.

Smith took over, "Pluto and Flash have something from the Fort." The National Security Agency at Fort Meade, Maryland had the finest linguists in America and it was clear "the Fort" had dedicated resources to this mission.

Pluto started, "On the bird into Bagram, we talked about the possible characters involved. It turns out that all the intercepts point to Din Mohammed as the kidnapper. He has already sent out a call to local warlords bragging that he has an American commando in custody and he said he sent a ransom note to the US consulate in Peshawar. About the same time, he received a call on his Thuraya from an unknown Thuraya satellite phone which was previously linked to a Haqqani support network in Nangarhar. One of the confusing bits of data is another Thuraya target of interest regarding Jameson appears to be Uzbeks or Chechens involved and led by a guy called Ruslam Yekdast. It looks like Yekdast negotiated a deal by offering twice what Din Mohammed wanted for Jameson. In short, we have lost the ransom negotiation and now Din Mohammed is just waiting for Yekdast to come to his compound, give him the money and take Jameson to some other location."

Smith looked at Jamie, "You have any local sources that we can leverage today to give us more information on the compound, Din Mohammed or any of this?"

Jamie nodded, "We have a couple of cross-border assets that we have already tasked. Two meetings scheduled for tonight. I figured Wally would take one and I would take the other."

Smith nodded, "I want our folks in the game, Jamie."

"Never thought otherwise, Colonel. I can take Sue and Wally can take your other guy."

"Hey, that other guy is me. You can call me Doug or you can call me Pigpen." Just like Sue, Pigpen was tired of being wallpaper in the TOC.

Wally looked at him and said, "Pigpen, you want to come, you get to come. We are meeting BLASTFURNACE, a Mohmand tribal from the Konar side of the border. You speak the lingo?"

"Nope, but if you need a scribe and a second set of eyes on your target, I'm your man."

Massoni chimed in, "Sue, I seem to remember you know some Dari from our time in J-bad, right?"

Sue had been reluctant to offer her language skill up to the group because she hadn't practiced it since Jalalabad in '03, but she knew she needed to answer. "I'm rusty but can certainly serve as Jamie's backup so long as he doesn't speak too fast."

Jamie chimed in, "My source, NICKLETRUE, is a Mohmand Pushtun with the same level of Afghan Dari as mine. I suspect you will be able to keep up." Jamie paused, "Colonel, the ODA commander wants to know if we need his team for the operation. I defer to you, but I would recommend we use them as a blocking force in case some or all of our targets make a run for the Konar."

Smith nodded, "Makes sense to me. Jim, you and I need to talk to the ODA commander, figure out what he can and can't do for us and then get him to agree." Smith turned to Jamie, "Is the ODA commander a mother may I guy or a better to beg forgiveness rather than ask permission guy?"

Jamie shrugged. "I think in this case, he is going to just do what you tell him to do. The word already came down from Bagram and from Special Forces Command at Bragg that anything you need, you get. You have some juice both as a colonel and as a SOF senior. I don't think he is going to mouth off."

Massoni jumped into his Sergeant Major role. "That's the ticket" he said. "OK, folks. Here's the deal. I can see that Wally, Pluto and Flash haven't had sleep in at least 24 hours. You guys need to put your heads down for a couple of hours. Pigpen and Sue, you need to do the same. The boss and I will work with Jamie for two hours, wake up Sue and Pigpen for the next rotation and put our heads down. We will all be ready to roll at 1600hrs for a long, cold night on the border. Check?" Everyone nodded. Pluto and Flash closed their laptops down and followed Sue and Pigpen to the barracks.

Jamie, Wally, Massoni, Flash, Pigpen and Sue, half of Jamie's commandos, and six Green Berets from the SF ODA moved forward to another small compound on the Afghan border at dusk. They travelled in two ancient, ten-ton cargo trucks. The plan was to move to a rendezvous patrol base with other Tomahawks. At that point, Jamie, Wally, Sue and Pigpen would move on horseback from the base camp to the two meeting sites for the OGA sources. After the meeting, they would check in with Smith and Pluto at FOB Pech to get the latest from Kabul, Bagram and "the Fort." Flash had insisted on going forward with the rest of the team. As she said, "You will need someone smart on call." Smith and Massoni didn't argue since she was already in the vehicle with her Remington sniper rifle when she announced her intention. If all went well, by midnight they would have a much better understanding of the situation and could decide both what to do next and when to do it. The SF operators who sat next to Flash clearly didn't know what to make of a female SOF sniper and Flash didn't help much by putting on her most serious game face when they tried to make nice with her.

The ride to the border outpost was a typical bit of third world madness. Sue always thought of "Mr. Toad's Wild Ride" from *Wind in the Willows* whenever she loaded into local vehicles driven by local drivers. The mix of chaos, terror, and rough roads kept the passengers awake and uncomfortable through the entire trip. This was especially the case when the drive was in pitch dark. The smugglers' road was little more than a donkey track but Jamie's drivers seemed to intuit the best possible route that prevented scraping the right side of the truck against the mountain faces or plunging down the cliff face to the local tributary of the Konar River. Sue was certain that if she had seen the route during daylight hours, she would have opted to walk behind the truck all the way to the border.

Once they arrived at their dismount point, the move from the patrol base to the meeting sites was an equally challenging trip. Jamie's Tomahawks had ponies ready on their arrival. Jamie and Sue left on a track heading North and Wally and Pigpen on a track headed South. Sue hadn't ridden since she lost her leg. The prosthetic on her left leg made mounting up difficult and getting her left boot in to the stirrup even more of a challenge. Flash helped by giving Sue a boost up and then leaned in and said, "Jamie is going to have to help you get down. He's a trustworthy Klingon so I wouldn't worry about letting him know."

Sue looked at Flash and asked, "So, Flash. What sort of experiments did you perform in Balad to confirm his trustworthiness."

Flash smiled and responded, "Girl, you know the deal. Chicks just don't ask and we also don't tell."

The ride was less than an hour. It seemed longer both because Sue had no idea where they were going and it was pitch dark. Jamie had attached a one inch chemical marking light to the back of his bearskin robe so Sue was following a ghostly green light that appeared to float twenty feet ahead. She had to trust the Afghan pony to keep on the trail since she couldn't see the trail or any hazards to the left or right. Later when they arrived, she found out that it was all for the best when Jamie said, "We just crossed a pass into Pakistan that I've only done once in the daylight. Honestly, it is better that you don't see the 200-foot drop that was to our left for most of the ride."

Sue asked Jamie to help her off the horse and when he did he felt the hard polymer that made up the prosthetic on her left leg. "Girl, you are hard as woodpecker lips. I knew you had some sort of trouble with your left leg when we were in Iraq, but I just assumed it was a knee or ankle problem like I have. A full up prosthetic and you are wandering in bandit country with me. I hope we don't have to run away tonight."

Sue turned and said, "Don't worry, Jamie. I won't leave you behind."

As they set up their small meeting site, Jamie took the chemical light off his robe and tied it to a tree ten yards in front of where they had their horses hobbled. The green glow now served as a beacon to NICKLETRUE while not revealing their location. Sue and Jamie sat in the dark waiting for the source. Neither needed to break the silence in their mountain location. A cold hour after they arrived, they heard NICKLETRUE. Jamie started a second, larger chemical light so their meeting site was bathed in a shallow, green glow. NICKLETRUE was dressed in a grey shalwar kamiz that made him nearly invisible in the moonlight. He was a tall Pashtun with a pencil thin mustache and a whisp of a grey beard dyed with henna which made it a strange mix of white, red and orange. He was wearing a leather shoulder holster paired to a leather ammunition belt which made a cross in the center of his chest. The holster had a revolver that probably arrived in the region during the British Raj. Attached to the ammunition belt was a Khyber knife. In his left hand, he held a World War II vintage, bolt action Enfield .303 rifle. Against the cold, he had a thick wool shawl wrapped around his shoulders. Sue shivered given the evidence that he appeared impervious to the cold.

Jamie whispered to Sue, "Keep an eye on his right hand. If he makes a move for either the knife or the pistol, make sure he ends up with a dirt sandwich tonight, ok?"

"So, control of your source is a bit of a challenge?"

"Hard to say, but I'm taking no chances. I will introduce you as my bodyguard if that's ok. It will prevent him giving you a hug and giving away your chickdom."

"Got it. I will listen and only speak if you ask."

"Thanks. Here goes." Jamie's white teeth under his enormous mustache beamed as he smiled and approached NICKLETRUE to give him a bear hug. Sue listened carefully and could follow the Dari with some ease because, as Jamie had said, neither he nor NICK-LETRUE spoke it fluently. Their dialogue was made up of simple, short sentences.

"My friend, thank you for coming."

"It is always a pleasure to see you, Mr. Candles. Who is your friend?"

"Abdul, this is Mason. He is my bodyguard tonight because I was bringing funds to thank you for helping. I hope you have something for me as well." Sue nodded, but stayed in the shadows.

"Mr. Candles, you asked about Din Mohammed's compound. I have brought a map." He pulled a crumpled piece of paper from his worn wool vest. Jamie took the paper in his right hand and offered a leather saddlebag to NICKLETRUE. Neither man looked at the "gifts" that were exchanged. Jamie and NICKLETRUE sat down on two flat rocks that faced each other divided by the green chemical light between them. From another saddlebag Jamie brought out a thermos and one tin cup. He poured liquid into the cup and Sue could smell the aroma of the strong sweet milky tea. Jamie handed the cup to NICKLETRUE who took a drink and handed it back to Jamie who drank some and handed it back to NICKLETRUE making sure the cup ended up in NICKLETRUE's right hand. Sue knew that this was partly cultural because you never offered food or drink from your "dirty" left hand to a "dirty" left hand, but she also knew NICKLETRUE would have to drop the cup before he reached for pistol or knife. By that time, Sue would have put three rounds in the Pashtun.

"Do you have any information on the man kidnapped by Din Mohammed? Who is he and where is he being held?"

"My friend, I think he is an American soldier, but I have not seen him. You always say I need to tell you what I think or what I know. I know Din Mohammed has a hostage and intends to sell him tomorrow night. I think he is an American simply because Din Mohammed's men say so."

"How many men are in Din Mohammed's compound?"

"Five armed men, his wife and children and the hostage. Of course, there are his relatives in the other compounds, but they don't like him so I don't think they would be much trouble."

Sue was concerned that Jamie was giving up too much to NICKLETRUE. It would be too easy for NICKLETRUE to sell their plans just as he sold Din Mohammed's plans. What Jamie said next made it clear that she didn't need to worry.

"You know you are going to take us to Din Mohammed's house?"

"Mr. Candle, I don't want to do this thing."

Jamie smiled his most engaging smile and said, "My friend, you will either do so or you will not leave here tonight." Jamie looked over at Sue.

"He can do this thing?"

"He has done this thing many times before just for me. I am sure of him."

"Then I have no choice."

"That is how I think."

"Is there a reward for my agreement?"

"Of course, we always pay well both in advance and afterwards. I have already provided double the normal pay in the saddlebag and will double it again for this work."

"And what makes you think I came alone tonight?"

"Our magic eye in the sky, same as always. It never sleeps, it can see in the dark, and as you know it can fire missiles."

"I have seen what they have done in the past. I know this to be true. We leave now?"

"Yes. I will leave first, you follow and Mason will follow you. This is acceptable?" NICKLETRUE nodded. As Jamie walked past Sue toward the horses, he winked and said, "I hope you followed that you are my muscle."

Sue nodded and said, "Right…muscle. Is he going to walk to the base?"

"Only as far are our pre-arranged departure point. My guys are waiting about a 30 minute walk away. You good for 30 minutes?"

Sue turned to Jamie as she picked up the second chemical light and handed it to him, "I reckon I can walk for a half hour. Lead on, Mr. Candles…"

"I will be your light." Jamie's brilliant white teeth below the mustache flashed again as he pulled the chem light from the tree, attached the second chem light to the same string and started walking his pony down the trail.

They assembled at a collapsed house compound on the ridge line above the Din Mohammed compound. Pigpen and Wally arrived with BLASTFURNACE, walking between them with flex cuffs on his hands and a sandbag over his head. Massoni, Flash, six Green Berets and six of Jamie's Tomahawks walked in from the West and Jamie, Sue and NICKLETRUE arrived from the South. Jamie parked NICKLETRUE outside the compound with Sue watching him. The sky was turning from jet black to dark purple as night turned into dawn. Flash looked at Pigpen and then at the hooded BLASTFURNACE. Pigpen shrugged his shoulders and said, "Later."

The plan was simple enough. They would enter the compound just before dawn when any night guards would be groggy. Jamie had NICKLETRUE's map of the compound and they hoped it would be possible to get Jameson without any gunplay. If they were successful, they would grab Jameson and they would GTFO. In Massoni's Ranger Regiment parlance that meant "Get The Fuck Out." Massoni would move with the six Green Berets and two of the Tomahawks into a blocking position overlooking the compound. Wally and Flash would be in overwatch and receiving voice from Smith and Pluto and data from the UAVs that were circling the target. Jamie would move to the compound with NICKLETRUE; Sue, Pigpen and the remaining Tomahawks would be in Ranger file behind Jamie. Flash set up the Remington and used a rangefinder to determine whether she could hit any targets in the compound. She turned to Massoni and said, "It is a thousand yards to the inside the compound. Jim, its more than I can do, especially in the dark. I can definitely cover on the way in and on the way back."

Massoni nodded and said, "That's more than we can expect from you, Flash. They shouldn't need any help on the way in and will count on your cover on their way out. If they need anything else, Wally needs to put a call to Jed to get the armed Pred out there." One of the UAVs was an armed Predator with two HELLFIRE missiles on board. The missiles would be able to reach out and touch someone as soon as Flash designated the target with the laser designator also strapped to the Remington. Massoni tapped Flash on the shoulder and said, "I'm going to move back up the ridgeline to set up the blocking force with the SF guys. I will be 5 on the net. Check?"

Sue knew that more than anyone Jim Massoni wanted to be in the compound when they rescued Jameson. However, she also knew that Smith was right when he said to Massoni back at the base, "Jim, I am staying here with Pluto in case we need more heavy support. You need to make sure we have closed the backdoor. I think the ODA needs a Sergeant Major to make it happen." Massoni just nodded then and he nodded now as he walked up the hill leading BLASTFURNACE by ten feet of nylon parachute cord attached to his wrists.

They started down the slope to the compound through a series of snow drifts that covered the eastern slope of the hillside. As they approached the compound, NICKLETRUE was in the lead followed by two of the Tomahawks, followed by Jamie. The remaining stars and the false dawn light reflected on the snow made it easy to descend from the hillside and join the smugglers' track that led to Din Mohammed's compound. As they pulled up on the tree line next to the walled compound, Sue noted the first obstacle to their search: a groggy guard leaning against the mud brick wall that served as the defensive perimeter of the compound as well as the fence keeping some of Din Mohammed's sheep safe from animal and human predators. Sue was surprised when she saw one of Jamie's men creep out of the tree line, pull out a tomahawk and throw it. The tomahawk made three revolutions and landed in the middle of the guard's head. The guard made no sound as he slid down from his bench at the entrance of the compound. Through the command net, the US team heard Jamie's voice say, *"One down. Entering now."*

Jamie, NICKLETRUE and two Tomahawks disappeared through the door that was just wide enough for a Toyota Hi-Lux pickup truck. The rest of the team waited along the edge of the wall. When Sue saw Jamie's outstretchd arm at the door with a thumbs up, she and Pigpen moved to the compound wall and stood next to the dead guard. Jamie's man had recovered his tomahawk, grabbed his Kalashnikov rifle and left the guard against the wall.

"Entrance clear. Second guard down. We are moving to where we think they have Jameson."

The team outside the wall moved in a stack through the entrance, matched up with Jamie, NICKLETRUE and the two Tomahawks. The full team now split into two sections moving along opposite walls of the compound.

Flash's voice came over the network, *"Standby, standby."* She paused to be sure everyone stopped and was listening. *"WATCHDOG to all. One of the preds just picked up Jameson's GPS signal moving away from the compound headed toward the border. The IR camera onboard the pred has identified two SUVs driving along the same track we came in on and another SUV with Jameson headed along the border on another track."*

Jamie held up his hand in a fist and took a knee. Everyone on the team did the same. He thought for a minute. Before he could say anything, Smith's voice came over the net and said, *"All, this is 6. We need more data before we start chasing our tails. TOMAHAWK team, do what you need to do inside the compound to confirm our package is not there. WATCH-DOG, we will inform higher that we want that Pred to track the GPS signal."*

Massoni's voice came on the network, *"Do you want us to intercept the convoy when they get across the border?"*

Smith responded *"5, your call. If you can conduct the intercept without any risk to our side, I say yes. If not, then not. It doesn't look like they are part of the play."*

"Roger, Roger. 5 out."

NICKLETRUE stayed at the gate with one of the Tomahawks while the team worked their way around the compound from opposite sides. Jamie and his Tomahawks headed toward the big house where they expected to find Din Mohammed. Pigpen and Sue headed to the small house, really not much larger than the standard outhouse in Central Asia, where they expected Jameson. They arrived to find the door open and the first light of dawn sending a shaft of grey into the house. Two of Din Mohammed's guards looked at them through opium clouded eyes. The guards tried to put their Kalashnikovs in action, but before they could reach their rifles, Pigpen and Sue had put three rounds in each man. Pigpen used his suppressed M4 carbine, Sue used her suppressed MP5. The only noise in the room was the sound of the bolts opening and closing and the cartridge casings hitting the dirt floor. Pigpen transmitted, *"All, two more down in the small house. No sign of Jameson."*

Jamie and his Shia fighters entered the main room of house where Din Mohammed and three more of his guards were drinking tea. The Tomahawks made quick work of the guards using bladed weapons. Jamie pointed his suppressed M4 carbine at the Pashtun tribal leader and shouted the only Pashtu he knew, "Harakat makawa!" which he had been told was "don't move" but, honestly, if it had been "Where are the apricots?" it probably would have worked just as well given Jamie's facial expression and the M4 pointed directly at Din Mohammed's forehead. Din Mohammed knew his life depended on obeying the intruder, at least for the time being. One of the Toma-hawks left the room in search of more Pashtuns to kill.

The other of the Tomahawks, who spoke Pashtu, walked over to Jamie and said in Dari, "What do you want him to tell you?"

Jamie responded easily, "Ask him where the American is being held." The exchange that followed seemed far more complicated than the answer that Jamie expected. Finally, he interrupted in Dari and asked his fighter, "What did he say?"

Din Mohammed had tired of the translation game, so he spoke directly to Jamie in crisp Pakistani-accented English. "I said, you are too late. A crew of Uzbeks came for your colleague and left. They paid up front, but also told me that they would kill me if I didn't give them the American."

Jamie pointed at Din Mohammed and told his fighter, "Use the flex cuffs and hood him." The fighter showed practiced precision and soon Din Mohammed was on the floor with his hands and ankles in nylon flex cuffs linked together by a single bit of wire. At that point, Pigpen and Sue entered the room.

"What's the story?" was all Sue said.

"The creep says he sold Jameson to the Uzbeks and they left."

"And you believe him?"

"I don't believe him now, but I will soon. Let's just go outside and regroup for a minute." Jamie turned to his fighter and said in Dari, "Tell him that we want to know truth or I will leave him with you." The fighter smiled and leaned over the hooded man and whispered in his ear a long monologue in Pushtu while Jamie, Wally, Pigpen and Sue left.

Pigpen spoke in his most official tone and said, "Shenk, the United States Army does not condone abuse of prisoners."

"Brother, we don't abuse anyone. However, we just might make the creep think that the Hazara are going to have some unsuper-vised fun with him. After all, we just killed his entire bodyguard, so he knows we are serious. It won't take long. The Tomahawks are very… persuasive."

"No blood, Shenk."

"No blood or marks. Just a whisper in his ear. In the meantime, you might want to tell your boss what we know. Don't ya think?" Pigpen nodded and left the building. As soon as he was out of the building, he sent the message on the net. Smith responded and told them all the data supported what they were seeing inside the compound.

About a minute later, the Tomahawk came out the door. He said in Dari, "That man says Uzbeks took him, but they split up. One set in two vehicles and one separate vehicle. He doesn't know anything else except he wants us to have the money they paid him. Just to be sure we are friends." The Hazara smiled. "And...he wants to give us this note he says came from Jameson." He handed the note to Jamie. Jamie looked at the note and passed it to Sue. It was addressed to "My daughter, Sue."

Sue walked back to the room. Din Mohammad was sitting up and no longer hooded. He was gagged and cuffed, but breathing normally with no sign of trauma. The Hazara leaned over to Sue and said in Dari, "He is very sad." He pointed to a bag in the corner. "He says money is in the bag." The Tomahawk walked toward the bag when Sue stopped him. She said in Dari, "Uzbeks left something bad in the bag. We leave the bag. Tell him we know he is a spy and the money will show it when his cousin comes for him." The Hazara smiled and nodded. Din Mohammed's eyes widened as the Tomahawk reiterated in Pashtu what Din Mohammed already understood in English.

"It is time to go," was all Sue said as she turned her back on Din Mohammed.

When she came out, the team was ready to leave. "No dough?" Jamie said with a smile.

"I thought we might just leave it with him. Either it has a booby trap in it or it shows everyone in town that he is a spy for someone. Works either way."

Jamie said, "Too true. And, anyhow, we were never here." He turned to Sue and said, "What's in the note?"

Sue said, "Probably some sort of coded message from Jameson. I reckon it will take more than a quick glance to sort it out. I will share it with you when we get out of here and when we can talk this through with Smith and Massoni."

Jamie nodded and started walking out of the compound. They met NICKLETRUE at the gate and started up the hill toward Flash.

About halfway up the hill, they heard Flash say, *"You got a pair of guys coming out of the compound. They look pretty pissed."* Jamie looked back. Just as he did, there was a muffled explosion from inside the main house and black smoke started to rise above the compound wall. For a moment, the pursuers stopped and looked back at the compound and then redoubled their effort running up the slope toward the team.

Jamie spoke to Flash in between deep breaths as he ran uphill through ankle deep snow, *"Hey, Flash. Ya think you could do something about these guys?"*

There was a pause in the communications. Flash had already set her sight on the trailing pursuer. Once she had the right sight picture, she pulled the trigger. The suppressor on the rifle reduced the muzzle flash and the sound. The man dropped face first into the snow. Flash worked the bolt action, reset her sight on the first pursuer and pulled the trigger. Again, the target dropped into the snow.

"Take look back downslope, Mr. Bear."

"No need. I heard the rounds as they went overhead."

"You can say thank you later. You don't have to run anymore. A guy your age could get a heart attack."

By the time they got to Flash's position, Wally had packed up the satcom rig, and put it in his ruck. Flash had shouldered her ruck and folded up the bipod on the rifle. She said, "I reckon we need to match up with Massoni. I heard some gunfire a couple of minutes ago and then nothing. I suppose there is nothing much to do, but we probably have something to work on now."

Jamie took the lead as they headed toward the border.

Jameson's move from the Din Mohammed compound had been quick and his handlers had made it clear they would prefer to kill him, but were apparently under some restraint from doing so. They grabbed him from Din Mohammed, threw flex cuffs on his wrists and a nylon hood over his head. They pushed him out the door and into a waiting vehicle. After a very short drive, they pulled him out of the vehicle, pulled the hood off his head, threw a blanket over his back and tied a red nylon climbing rope to his flex cuff and passed the rope between his legs. The end of the rope was controlled by a captor to his rear. Any resistance Jameson might manage and the rope would pull him off his feet as well as creating a fair bit of pain between his legs. The man in front of him started off down a well-worn footpath of ice and snow and the one behind pushed him forward to follow. He watched as the two vehicles pulled away on the track headed back into Afghanistan.

Jameson was glad for the blanket even if the walk wasn't more than a mile or two in the snow. It was "mountain cold" on the border with temperatures well below freezing and humidity barely 10 percent. He could watch his breath fog and circle behind him as he was pushed forward. In less than an hour, they came upon a main road and a waiting ten-ton cargo truck decorated from front to back with garish paintings. Even in the circumstances, Jameson had to smile as he identified pictures on the side of the truck of the Nina, Pinta and Santa Maria sailing ships of Columbus. Trucks on both sides of the border were decorated from top to bottom with garish paintings, usually from some Bollywood movie poster. Still, Christopher Columbus was a new logo. His captors didn't give him much time to enjoy the irony as they grabbed him by the wrists and ankles and threw him into the back of the truck. They climbed in behind him and the truck pulled out onto the road and headed West into the Pech valley.

Jameson thought about trying to make an escape at that point, but just as he began to settle into a position which would allow him to jump from the truck, one of his captors pulled on the rope sufficiently hard that it nearly dislocated Jameson's shoulders and sent his head into the floorboards of the truck. In addition to being left face down on the truckbed, the incident left a burning sensation in his groin and ended any plan to jump and run for it. Jameson couldn't tell if that was simply a bit of sadism on the part of the guy with the rope or if he had noticed Jameson shifting his position. Either way, all Jameson could think was "Well, that's going to leave a mark." He decided to rest and watch the winter sky turn from black, to deep blue, to slate gray as they drove into the morning light.

After two hours in the back of the freezing truck, Jameson realized they were pulling into a walled compound on the edge of a city. Based on time and what little sense of direction Jameson had from his vantage point in the back of the truck, he assumed the city was Asadabad, the provincial capital of Konar Province. Once inside the compound and once the large wooden gate was closed, the Chechens in the truck tossed Jameson out and onto the ground. He survived the six foot drop by completing a shoulder roll and recovering before the two men could get down and start to kick him.

"Well done, Chief Jameson. I see that you haven't lost your skills yet. I am very pleased to welcome you to your new home and even more pleased that my men haven't done you any real harm." Jameson looked up at the man who spoke in unaccented English. He was a lean, dark haired man in an expensive ski outfit in sky blue with red stripes along the sleeves. The man wore gloves and a knit hat with the Russian Federation flag running around the brim.

"I don't think my balls would agree," was all he could think of saying.

"Mr. Jameson, things could always be worse, don't you think?"

Just as he spoke the man pulled out a taser and stunned Jameson into unconsciousness.

It was a serious snowstorm outside with zero visibility and twenty mile an hour wind. Everyone and everything that could take shelter in the valley had done so. Inside the TOC, the tables were filled with maps, half empty cups, pencils, and laptops. Twenty years ago, the room would be filled with cigarette smoke. Now, the only odd smells were coming from the Special Forces team leader and his number two who were drinking one energy drink after another. So much so that the various chemical "energy" enhancers in the drinks were coming out their pores. In their part of the building there was probably more than one member of the team using some sort of smokeless tobacco, but Massoni had made it clear that was not welcome in *his* TOC. In typical Massoni fashion, he had taped a sign on the door which said "Worm Dirt Free Zone" and a circle with a slash through a can of snuff. No one messed with the Sergeant Major.

Sue was in a particularly deep funk. There were no leads that she could see to finding Jameson and she was trapped indoors in a blizzard. The note from Jameson had been more personal than anything else. The open code he used had only said that he expected to be picked up by a single outfit that paid Din Mohammed to conduct the kidnapping and bring him to the border. The rest of the note had been a farewell letter that only made Sue want to cry like a baby. So far, she had resisted tears, but it wasn't easy.

The SF team with Massoni's guidance had conducted a kinetic ambush on the convoy about one hundred meters inside Afghanistan. They didn't use any explosives in the ambush so the vehicles and one of the occupants survived. No Jameson and nothing to point to where he had gone. Adding to the complication, the "pocket litter" found on the occupants showed they were not Uzbeks at all but Chechens. Sue couldn't see a way clear to do anything.

Pluto finally broke the silence in the room and said, "Uzbek extremists from the Islamic Movement of Afghanistan have been living in Afghanistan and in the Pakistan tribal areas for years. They have intermarried with the Waziris and the Mahsuds down in Waziristan and live among the Pakistani extremists and drug lords. They are accepted foreigners. Chechens, on the other hand, have been fighters for hire for Al Qaida and don't really have a home here. Honestly, they don't have a home anywhere anymore ever since Putin's scorched-earth policy in the Caucasus in 1999. Extremists for sure, but not locals. Beats me why they are here."

Once again, Flash demonstrated an additional skill set that she hadn't shared with Sue. She asked Smith, "Can I question our single prisoner?"

Smith smiled, "Flash, you speak Russian?"

"Boss, you know I do. Long before our pal Sue arrived, you had me working a case in Kosovo sorting out "good Russians" from "bad Russians.""

"And all you could tell me then was they were all bad. Not a ton of Russian language needed for that analysis."

Flash smiled a Cheshire cat smile, "It was the truth, but it took real linguistic skill to prove it."

The SF captain spoke up for the first time. "Colonel, one of my guys is a 4 level Russian speaker. Senior NCO who has been in 10th since Bad Tolz. He could help."

Massoni slapped the Captain on the back so hard, he spilled his energy drink down the front of his uniform. "Captain, now we are in business. Let's see what a 4 level speaker does with our man…er, woman, Flash. We need some sort of lead, any lead will do."

The Captain went back to his side of the compound and returned with his man. Flash grabbed the senior NCO by the arm and they headed to where the Chechen fighter was being detained. The Captain also brought the team medic since the fighter was wounded in the ambush. He turned to Flash and said, "I'm not used to working with SOF Klingons but I have been here long enough in Castle Shenk to know that we may need a medic along."

Jamie was already in his "bear suit." He responded, "So unfair, young Captain. I never hurt anyone in my custody."

"And your Hazaras?"

"I don't know, you will have to ask them."

"You know I don't speak Dari."

"Then ask me and I will be the translator."

"The last time I did that, the conversation went on for about ten minutes before you gave me a one-word answer to my question. That answer was simply no."

"It's a complicated language with lots of ways of saying simple stuff."

Sue watched as they walked across the compound through ankle deep newly fallen snow. Their tracks started to fill up almost immediately with the heavy snowfall. Sue looked out the door and watched as they slowly disappeared into the storm.

They came back 90 minutes later. Flash shook off her Gore-Tex coat but kept her fleece jacket on. "Sheesh, it is cold out there and pretty darn cold in the cell."

Jamie was hanging up his fur coat and said, "It is not a cell, it is an apartment. Also, I told you that I could get a bear suit made just for you."

Flash ignored Jamie's offer and said to the team, "It is an apartment with a cot, a bucket of water and a bucket of waste."

"The SF guys are going to transfer him to J-bad as soon as we can get a helo. He can have luxury accommodations then. My house, my choice. By the way, the SF guys don't want Mr. Stinky in their quarters and if I put him in with the Tomahawks." Jamie paused. He smiled and continued, "Well, I guess that might be a solution."

Smith and Sue were both fed up with the banter. Smith jumped in first, "And what precisely did you learn, Flash?"

"Boss, the Chechen said he and his pals were just hired guns for this Russian dude who was in the region smuggling old Soviet weapons to the Taliban and drugs back into the 'stans."

"Russian?" Sue wasn't really surprised since the intelligence stream for years had suggested that some Central Asian states were serving as platforms for Russian oligarchs to do precisely this sort of bilateral trade. Still, it was a long way from gun and drug smuggling to kidnapping an American.

"Yup. I hate to tell you this, Sue, but the Russian only has one hand."

Sue went pale. Jamie didn't know why so he just interjected his own view, "I wasn't real surprised. Yekdast just means one hand in Persian and it would be easy for an Afghan guy with wax in his ears to confuse Ruslam with Rusi."

Massoni was standing behind Sue and looking directly at Jamie. He made a throat cutting hand gesture to get Jamie to shut up. Jamie got the message and walked over to the coffee pot. As he passed Flash, he mumbled, "Was it something I said?"

Flash whispered back, "Dude, it is a long story."

Sue sat down with a thump on one of the metal folding chairs and said, "He's dead. I saw him die."

Smith walked over to Sue and sat down next to her. He said quietly, "Perhaps you only saw what he wanted to you see or the Russians wanted you to see. It is what we do after all."

"But why Bill Jameson?"

Massoni turned to Smith and said, "Why, indeed?" They didn't have to wait long to find out.

The snow storm stopped about midnight and they woke to a winter wonderland of snow-capped mountains, eighteen inches of snow on the helicopter LZ and temperatures near zero Fahrenheit. The wind had stopped before the snow drifted over the windows in the FOB. Massoni came down from his room to make coffee at 0500hrs and found Sue slumped over her computer. She was sleeping, but Massoni recognized the restless sleep she was having. He had his fair share of nightmares generated by years of combat and as a Sergeant Major he had counselled more SOF operators than he liked to count about "the dream."

Massoni's "dream" was always the same: He was in a war zone. Sometimes familiar, sometimes completely unfamiliar. Someone needed his help, bullets were flying everywhere but hitting nobody that he could see. The wounded were located someplace out of his field of vision and were crying out for help. He couldn't find his weapon or his boots or his clothes and he couldn't get there in time no matter how hard he tried. The dream could last for minutes or hours until he woke up soaked in sweat. He could wash off and try to get back to sleep. If he did, he would fall right back into the dream, only in another place and missing another item which prevented him from helping comrades. After nearly twenty years of working "down-range" in combat zones, some known, some secret, Massoni had just accepted the dream as part of warrior life. It was no different from the various aches and pains that reminded him of years of heavy rucksacks and hard parachute landings.

Massoni walked behind Sue and kicked her chair to wake her up.

He knew that downrange, an operator might wake with a knife or gun in hand; Massoni didn't want to have to do harm to Sue just to avoid a dirt sandwich. He definitely didn't want to tangle with Sue after "the dream." He didn't use his parade ground voice, but he did put an edge to his instruction when he said, "Sue, you need to get up, get cleaned up and come back down for some breakfast. Now, O'Connell."

Sue wiped the drool from her mouth and blinked twice. She had been suffering through the dream again and, yet, the dream was morphing into reality as she remembered that Jameson was still missing and she was still clueless how she could help.

"Jim, we need to get to work. We have to find the Chief."

Massoni nodded, smiled and said, "Right now you need to get cleaned up and start the day fresh. You are still carrying about two days worth of schmutzig on your body and nobody wants to work with you in that condition. Especially me."

Sue looked down at her uniform and realized that Massoni was right. "Check, Sergeant Major. Back in 15 with a clean body, a clean uniform and ready for coffee."

"Make it 20 and you're on." Massoni knew sooner or later, and he hoped it was sooner, there would be a breakthrough and they would all have to go to the red line of their capabilities to save his friend Bill Jameson. As the senior NCO in this effort, he had to keep his people as healthy and as fresh as possible. He had forced everyone to bed the previous night, but obviously Sue had snuck down to the TOC after hours and decided looking over the same data for the twentieth time was somehow going to help. Massoni knew it didn't. He caught Smith trying at 0330hrs and chased him back to bed. Massoni tried on his own at 0430hrs with no luck. Instead, he opted for twenty minutes of tai chi, pushups, and situps and a shower. When he arrived to find Sue at the computer, he felt better though no less concerned.

The sky was turning a light blue-gray in what civilians might call false dawn and soldiers, Marines, sailors and airmen call BMNT – begin morning nautical twilight. It is the time when soldiers in combat from all countries are called to "stand to" because before night vision goggles it was the time when enemy raids took place.

Massoni watched as Jamie started his rounds taking tea to his watch standers, waking his remaining Tomahawks and insuring they would be ready to go when/if the US team decided to move out. Upstairs in the living quarters, Flash looked out from her window to see "Jamie the bear" working his way through the snow delivering tea. She smiled at the image. Her time with Jamie in Iraq had been brief but enjoyable. She wondered if there would be a time when she could meet him in someplace other than a warzone. "Not anytime soon, kid," was all she said to herself.

In another part of the compound, the full SF team woke at 0530hrs for stand to and to plan for the day's work. Over breakfast, they would share the results of the previous day and outline what they were going to do today. Though an interesting distraction from their regular routine, the SOF and OGA mission was only part of their warzone duties. It would be a busy day if the sky remained clear. They would need to clear the landing zone so they could get an Army helicopter into the FOB to transfer the Chechen to Jalalabad. After that, half of the team would walk down to the local village to continue their VSO training. The other half of the team would spend their day cleaning equipment, writing reports and generally planning for tomorrow and the next day and the next for the remainder of their 120-day tour in the FOB.

In the TOC, Massoni had used the quiet time to boil water for coffee, tea, and instant oatmeal. Smith was the first to arrive, clean shaven, showered and ready to start the day. As each team member returned to the TOC, Massoni insisted they eat something. He reminded them that once they got crazy busy, they might not have time for their next meal. By 0600hrs, everyone was in the TOC with a coffee cup in hand and some oatmeal down their throat.

Smith took charge, "With some luck, once we get the morning satellite cast in we will have more data to work with and we can start narrowing the search area. Last night before we lost comms, I heard from Bagram. They will have two UAVs in orbit as soon as the weather clears down in Jalalabad, probably in the next hour. They offered a little bird for us to use, but I think that will let everyone know we are looking and they will play hide and seek. I think electronic surveillance will be the key."

Wally offered, "I think BLASTFURNACE should be able to narrow the search area down. He is a wiley cat and I suspect he always knows more than he says. A little financial inducement coupled with some threats and I hope he gives us something we can use. When we released him last night, he headed home to Asadabad. We need to see him again."

Flash said, "If he is so damn smart, how come he didn't help in Mohmand country and why did you bag and tag him on the border?"

Wally countered, "He isn't a Mohmand and didn't know shit when it came to Din Mohammed. Once I realized that, I decided he had to be detained until we did our thing."

Jamie agreed, "BLASTFURNACE is the man when it comes to smuggling routes and his ability to get information with the right sort of financial inducement."

Flash looked at Jamie. "Inducement? Is that what you call it?"

"Sometimes…" was all he said in reply.

Smith looked at Pigpen and said, "Once Wally gets the meeting, go help him and come back with something useful, check?"

"Yes sir." Pigpen was certain that for this operation, his skills from his former job as a SOF shooter were probably more useful than his skills as a HUMINT operator without language. Still, whatever the boss wanted was what Pigpen wanted to deliver.

Smith stood up and said, "Jamie, can the Tomahawks do man-tracking in this snow?"

Jamie nodded. "I already dispatched a three-man team yesterday before the snow storm. They have HF radios and will call in as soon as they can find something useful. I told them to return by tonight if they didn't get a track."

Smith turned to the rest of the crew, "The rest of us will work on the intel as soon as we get the next cast which is…" he looked at his large GMT watch with registers on both local and Zulu time, "in 30 minutes if our communicators will just do their job."

Wally and Pluto stood up so fast their chairs went skidding across the TOC. They were out the door as soon as they could pull on their parkas. They climbed up on the roof and used their surefire flash-lights to find the satellite antennas. There were three on the roof, one for OGA, one for 171, and one for the Special Forces detachment. The snow and the wind had pushed the antennas over and the SF antenna was in a snow drift on the side of the building. Each of the teams had a specific time that they could transmit and receive satellite data signals known as their "cast," as in a "broadcast." However, if the dishes were covered with snow or dirt, it didn't matter when the signal was transmitted, they weren't going to receive it. After they cleared the dishes, Wally pulled out a compass and he and Pluto reset the dishes to acquire the communications satellites in geosynchro-nous orbit over Afghanistan. Wally looked at his digital watch and said, "Just in time for us to get down and start to pull in the cast." Pluto nodded and they climbed down the ladder and walked back into the TOC.

The transmissions from Bagram and from Kabul Station were helpful but not the breakthroughs that the team had hoped for at breakfast. The SOF UAV feeds did pick up the point where the Chechen convoy stopped and three men, including one in handcuffs, headed south on foot along the Pakistan-Afghan border. Since the tasking had been to track the convoy, the autonomous sensor package had done just that and the bird had a very good tape of the ambush and the SF and Massoni capturing the Chechen. Kabul station, work-ing with the Afghan National Directorate of Security had captured a cellphone message from the same general region. The two callers talked about a linkup site along the border where they would transfer the "package" to a truck. Helpful, but until they got a lead on where the truck was or where it went, it was not going to be very useful.

Jamie came into the TOC just as everyone was at the most depressed. He said, "The trackers found where the truck picked up our man. Definitely three men, all walking without difficulty. The team is still looking around for more details. I have the coordinates. It looks like they headed back into the Konar." He handed the GPS coordinates to Pluto who plotted them on a large 1:50,000 map of the area. The map covered most of one of the walls of the TOC. The coordinates showed the linkup with the truck hadn't been more than a mile from the drop-off point.

"What now?" was all Sue could say. They were chasing Jameson, he was still alive as of last night, but where was he now?

Wally swiveled his chair from his work station where the OGA communications gear covered most of the outside wall. "Jamie, you need to hear this. The guys have found something."

After a minute of listening and responding in Dari on the radio, he turned to the team and said, "They found a note nailed to a tree where the transfer took place. The Tomahawks can't read English. They did spell out what was on the outside of the note. I think it says, *Deliver to Susan O'Connell*. They are coming back to a coordinate where I will have them recovered by one of our off-road Polaris quad-bikes. They should be here in about an hour."

Sue stood up and said, "I'm going out with the quad-bikes. We don't have an hour to waste."

Smith grabbed Sue by the shoulder and forcibly made her return to her seat. "O'Connell, if this is the sort of note I think it is, we can't afford to run toward the trouble. At least, not yet. We need to have a plan and we need to work as a team." He spun Sue around on the chair so she was facing Smith and Massoni. "Check, O'Connell?!"

Sue realized that no matter how hard she wanted to run out the door, Smith was right. This was some sort of planned operation, some sort of complex chess game, and the only way to save Jameson's life was to work as part of the team in FOB Pech. Screwy, indeed.

Wally generated an emergency meeting with BLASTFURNACE. After he received confirmation from a satellite signaling device, he, Pigpen and two of the Tomahawks left at 2000hrs in an old military vehicle probably delivered to Afghanistan in the last years of the Soviet occupation before they left in 1989. They were going to meet the asset in a shepherd's cabin between Asadabad and the Afghan border with Pakistan. The meeting was set for 2300hrs and, if all went well, they would return at 0100hrs.

Winter weather had closed in again about an hour after Wally and Pigpen left. There was little that anyone could do until the snowstorm quit pelting the building with a mix of snow and sleet. Once again, the satellite dishes would have to be cleared of snow. Massoni walked over to Smith, Sue, Flash and Pluto and said, "I'm going to expect you to put some chow down your throats and get your heads down for an hour. There is nothing we can do now until we hear back from Jamie's crew and from Wally and Pigpen. After that, we are going to be running on adrenaline for a while."

Flash and Pluto both nodded to Massoni and headed to their bunks upstairs. Smith beat them upstairs, he knew you didn't argue with a sergeant major. Sue knew she couldn't sleep but she could eat and walked over to the kitchen to make herself a peanut butter sandwich and pour herself a glass of irradiated milk that arrived at the FOB on the weekly supply run from Jalalabad. She sat down next to Massoni and Jamie. Massoni was drinking coffee and Jamie a mug of very black tea.

"You guys going to go to bed?"

They said in unison, "Nope."

"You want to talk?"

Jamie said, "Nope."

Massoni said, "Sure."

Sue turned to Jamie and said, "If I talk to Jim, will it disturb your sullen mood?"

Jamie smiled, "Nope."

Sue turned to Massoni and said, "What do you think is going on, Jim? What are Bill's chances?"

"Sue, I think Bill's chances are excellent now that we know that this is part of some larger game. It is most probably part of the O'Connell vendetta which makes it a dangerous game, but until we know more, I don't think we can or should worry about Bill. And remember, he still might try to escape on his own."

Jamie asked, "What the heck is this O'Connell vendetta?"

Sue shook her head, "Long story, brother. It is about a family of spies in the US and a family of spies in Russia and a multi-generational fight between them."

Jamie rolled his eyes, "Look, I may seem like a simple knuckle dragger who is also running a multi-million dollar effort to undermine AQ here in the Konar, but please don't think I'm going to buy into a story like that."

Massoni reached out and touched Jamie's arm. "Really, Jamie. She is telling the truth."

"Now I know it is a gag if Massoni is going to vouch for it."

Sue interjected as she heard her voice almost break, "It is the real deal, Jamie. I didn't believe it myself until I was pushed into the trunk of a car that was rigged with explosives simply because my Russian counterpart is determined to give me a dirt sandwich. Oh, and by the way, he has a prosthetic hand because of a wound he got in Chechnya."

Jamie ran his right hand over his enormous mustache. "So, Jameson's kidnapping is an effort to use him as bait to get you near enough to kill."

"Well, I guess so. I thought we killed him months ago, but I suppose he's just hard to kill."

"Use a tantalum doorknocker. Works first time." Jamie said referring to the Hellfire missiles fired from the armed UAVs.

"I should have but I was in Cyprus and Russian commandos were shooting at me and, I thought, him. It might have been a stretch to get a UAV on station."

"So, he's not in the Russian service?"

"Russian mafia."

"Oh, perfect."

At midnight, Smith, Pluto and Flash came downstairs to find Sue, Massoni and Jamie head down at the table. Smith took the opportunity to use his own "parade ground voice" to wake them up. He shouted, "No drooling on my tables!"

The three jolted awake. Sue even came to the position of attention knocking over a chair and pushing about an inch of paper off the table and onto the floor. Flash was the first to stop laughing. "So, O'Connell, what sort of dream were you having that you had to come to the position of attention?"

Worried though Sue was, she smiled, "Back in Warrant Officer School at Ft. Rucker. A far better dream than I usually have."

Everyone on the team stayed up to get the news from these Hazara fighters who braved the weather and hostile tribals to deliver whatever message they carried. The Tomahawks arrived at the FOB near midnight. They were tired, hungry and cold. Jamie had already made them a pot of rice pilau and kebabs and pots of strong tea, so they recovered quickly. He came back to the TOC shortly after the arrival of Wally and Pigpen.

The debriefings started immediately with Smith in charge. "I need to hear both of the reports, but in order, please. Wally, what did BLASTFURNACE have to say?"

"He said that the word in the valley was that the Russian took Jameson and moved him to a compound in Asadabad. I know that sounds nuts since it means they are closer to us than anytime in the last 48 hours, but he insisted that he knew men who saw the Russian drive into a compound in the city."

Jameson woke and stared at the ceiling. The TASER shouldn't have knocked him out that thoroughly. He wondered what drugs they had used, but he didn't have the groggy feeling that one has coming out of an anesthetic. In fact, he was clear headed and that meant it was time to "check all the parts." First, he tried to move his hands and feet. All good which meant no spinal injury. Check. He sat up. No dizziness so far. Check. He was wearing a set of sky blue sweats with the Russian federation flag on the chest. Underneath the sweats were a striped t-shirt and a pair of gym shorts which the SOF community called "Ranger panties." He still had his dive watch which showed it was 0625hrs. He was barefoot. At the foot of the bed were a new pair of plastic flip flops. No boots in the room. Shit. Jameson thought "I'm inside, I'm alive and they still haven't tried to kill me. I suppose it is a good sign,"

He looked around the room. While not exactly a luxury hotel room, it was furnished like a residential bedroom not a cell. There was only one window on the opposite wall. It was delivering morning light, but too small to crawl out. Across from the single bed were a desk and chair and a open door. He could see that the door led to a small bathroom. He stood up, slipped his feet into the flip flops and tried walking across the room to the bathroom. A bit of stiffness and muscle pain you would expect from the shock of the TASER, but otherwise fine. He walked into the bathroom and found a kit with tooth brush, tooth paste, a plastic razor and a small can of shaving cream. No shower, but the sink had hot and cold running water, so Jameson decided to get cleaned up.

He had finished all of the necessary morning ablutions when he heard a knock on the door. All he could think was "Polite hostage takers. How refreshing." What he said was "Come in."

The man who walked in was the same one he had seen when he arrived. This time, he was dressed exactly the same as Jameson except instead of flip flops he was wearing lightweight combat boots. A little over six feet tall, definitely fit and Jameson noticed a prosthetic hand on his left arm. "Chief Jameson, my name is Nicolai Beroslav. I hope you found everything necessary to make for a pleasant stay."

"My Glock pistol would be useful."

"No doubt and I promise to deliver it to you at the proper time if all goes well. You see I want you to understand that I hope we can spend some quality time together before I return you to your command. I have no intention of holding you hostage nor do I want anything from you but a small degree of cooperation so that I don't have to restrain you before you are set free."

Jameson reached up and rubbed his head from back to front covering what little stubble was there. "What I would like to know first is how you kept me unconscious after the taser."

Beroslav laughed. "Russian Special Services secret. I can't reveal it to anyone outside the guild. The short answer is it is an acupressure technique that allows you to be rendered unconscious or, in extremis, killed without leaving a mark. Very useful and far better than any drugs that I could have used."

"Any chance of something to eat?" Jameson was still not sure what was going on and he figured food might be a good place to start.

"Certainly. It is morning, so I thought we could share breakfast. Here in the Konar, breakfast tends to be nothing more than some sort of porridge, flat bread and tea, but I suspect you have had worse fare in the last few days." Beroslav turned back to the open door and two guards entered. One was carrying a tray with the food and teapot. The other stayed just inside the doorway with a Skorpion machine pistol aimed at Jameson's chest. Both looked Central Asian and both had the look of killers.

Beroslav nodded to this guard. "Just a precaution in case you decided not to hear me out over breakfast."

"I got the picture pretty quickly." Jameson smiled and nodded to both of the guards. They didn't respond and kept their eyes focused on Jameson's chest and hands. If there would be trouble, they knew it would come from there. Jameson looked down at the table placed so that he could sit on his bed and eat.

Beroslav pulled up the desk chair and sat across from him. He poured two cups of tea into Russian style glasses, picked up one of the sugar cubes, put it in his mouth and started to drink the tea. He said with a smile, "I assumed you wanted to see me eat and drink first so that you know I'm not going to poison you."

"It did cross my mind. Also, I think the guards can leave now."

"No chance of that Chief Jameson. You might be able to take me out and might even take one of my two bodyguards out, but I promise you that you wouldn't be able to take all three of us or the two others still in the hallway. They have already had their breakfast, so don't be shy about having food with me." Jameson opened the covered bowl in front of him and found an apricot porridge and a small plastic spoon. He pulled apart some of the Afghan flat bread and started to eat. Beroslav did the same.

Beroslav opened the conversation when they were half finished. Jameson stopped eating and listened carefully.

S ue was like a caged lion, pacing back and forth from stairwell to
windows in the entrance way of the FOB watching the storm
rage outside. A late winter storm in the Konar was guaranteed to be severe and they were absolutely trapped in the compound.
None of the vehicles could traverse the snow drifts that were covering
the roads and until the snow stopped it would be impossible to use
either the quad-bikes or the horses on the foot trails to Asadabad.
The note the Tomahawks had found simply said "Asadabad" which
was unhelpful since they arlready knew from BLASTFURNACE that
their target location was now Asadabad. Worst of all, they were completely out of communication with the outside world. They couldn't
send or receive message traffic nor could they receive any feed from
the UAVs that would be circling over Asadabad...assuming they could
fly in the weather and see the ground. It was dark, it was frigid outside, the dampness and cold inside the TOC made her leg wound
ache and caused her prosthetic to fit poorly. And, there was nothing
she could do about anything. Sue was seriously pissed off. She had
been tossed out of the TOC for nagging Jamie and Wally every ten
minutes about the weather, the lack of communications and the fact
that they didn't know when they could head toward Asadabad. Sue
wanted news, any news and NOW. After a bit, Smith told her she
could just wait outside the TOC and they would tell her as soon as
they had any news.

Massoni came down the hall from the TOC. The arrival of Massoni in the large hall at the base of the stairs leading to the sleeping
quarters meant something was up. Sue wasn't sure if it would be

good news or bad news, but at least it would be news. Sue stopped pacing. "We got an HF radio signal from the Jalalabad TOC. It looks like the weather is going to break for us in the next six hours. We are putting together a plan. Smith says you can join us if you are on your best behavior. I warned him that you would be a snot, but he ordered me to bring you back into the TOC. Try your best to listen first before you talk. Get it?!" The last comment was delivered in Massoni's rare, "I'm a Command Sergeant Major" tone. Sue got the message.

"Check, Jim. I will keep silent unless I am asked a question."

"Sue, if you do that, people will think you have been possessed by some evil mountain spirit. I just want you to go with the flow. K?" Massoni turned and walked down the hall. Sue followed him.

Jamie was the first to greet Sue. "No hard feelings, Sue." He paused and said, "By the way, Flash made me say that. I really intend to hold a grudge." Sue stuck her tongue out at Jamie. Flash handed Sue a cup of tea. Sue could smell the chamomile and nearly threw it at Flash. Massoni gave Sue a look and she sat down and started to drink the herb tea.

Smith took charge of the briefing. "Here is what we know so far. It looks like we can start moving toward Asadabad at first light. Jamie and the Tomahawks will come with us and we will head toward a safehouse that Wally has just East of the city. We will set up there, reestablish communications and start the next steps of planning. Wally has a support agent there who can get us what we need. At this point, we don't know shit about what has happened or is happening in the compound in Asadabad, but best guess is the HF message would have said something if there was anything to say. Once we are in Asadabad proper, we will trigger a meeting with a 171 agent, 375. Sue, you and Pigpen will meet with 375 to see what, if anything, he has to say about Jameson."

Jamie turned to Sue and said, "You can thank Wally anytime you like for establishing the HF link as well as sending and receiving message traffic via morse code. I never thought it would come in handy, but between Wally, Massoni and yours truly, we were able to send and receive at ten words a minute. Not enough to pass an SF commo test, but enough to get things done."

Flash looked up and said, "I think I heard of morse code. Something to do with dots and dashes, right?" Massoni threw an empty Styrofoam cup at her.

Pluto said to no one in particular, "375 is our reporting source on extremist safehouses and cells in the Konar valley. He should be able to tell us something."

Jamie said, "Inshallah."

Smith stood up from the planning table to get back in command. "We are going to leave the ODA here in case there are any problems at our end. They will be a solid QRF for us once the skies clear and helicopters can land. They will only be 30 minutes out by helo." Smith nodded to the ODA commander who responded, "Check, sir."

Jamie took over, "Our travel down to Asadabad will be on horseback when we can and on foot when we have to. The Tomahawks know the passes and they will take us on the shortest, safest route. If the message is correct, we have about 48 hours before the next storm comes in. We need to be in the Pech River valley proper and heading to Wally's safehouse soon. One thing is certain, we are going to spend at least one night on the trail."

Massoni chimed in, "Camping, I love camping."

Pigpen responded, "Sergeant Major, we are not all as tough as you. Winter camping doesn't sound like a lot of fun."

Pluto said in his whisper voice, "I hate camping. Too many bugs."

Jamie decided to enter the fray, "NO BUGS in Winter camping. Just snow caves, a little primus stove, some Ranger school cocoa, and a good night's sleep under the stars. What's not to like?"

Smith ended the briefing by bringing the team back on message, "The basic plan is to get down to Asadabad, conduct an ad hoc surveillance of the target location, find out what we can from 375, and eventually determine if we can do the needful with the resources we have. If not, we whistle up the SOF raid team stationed in J-bad or the SF ODA here and wait for them to do what they do best." He paused to take a sip of tea. Sue noticed it wasn't chamomile tea. "Pack your rucks now with some winter kit from Jamie's stores, ammo, food and water. Wake up call will be 0500hrs, breakfast and then on the trail by 0630hrs."

"Pack extra socks," was all Massoni had to add.

The morning was clear and frigid. Over breakfast, Jamie let everyone know that the outside temperature was -10F. He also said with a smile that the good news was according to the Jalalabad base weathermen, the high should reach just above freezing. He said, "It is spring after all!" The Tomahawks prepared three horses to carry the equipment and four with saddles. They had three Polaris quad bikes already warmed up by the time they were outside. Jamie explained the operational plan for the day, "We are heading almost due South for about five miles to find the trail. Once we get on the trail, we head West until we hit the River Pech. That will be the end of the trail for today because by that time it will be dark and we really don't want to fall into the river when the air temperature is below freezing. We will rotate horseback, quad-bikes and walking. We just don't have enough transportation for the full team and the Tomahawks. Half the Tomahawks will take the lead on foot and half will pull rear guard. Remember, we are definitely in bad guy country so we can't assume that the biggest challenge today is going the distance. The cargo horses have a fur coat for each of you that will serve as ground cloth, blanket and, if the weather turns bad, your outside layer. Wally and I have ours already on one of the quad bikes and the Tomahawks carry theirs on their backs. Colonel Smith, any questions or additional instructions?"

Smith turned to Massoni, Pigpen, Pluto, Flash and Sue. "Massoni, Pluto and Sue, you start on the horses. We change out in two hours. I reckon we need to make sure Massoni's horse doesn't collapse under stress from his weight, so, when we rotate, Flash will take his horse, Pigpen will take Sue's. I will grab a ride on Pluto's horse. Wally and Jamie switch out between the last horse and a quad-bike as they work with the Tomahawks. We let the Tomahawks stay on the the remaning pair of quads since they know the trail. I don't need anyone upside down under a quarter ton of bike." Smith looked at the team, "Check?"

Massoni looked up to the sky and said, "Always the jokes about my weight. I'm a perfect 100 kilos. How can that be a bad thing?"

It was early, they hadn't had much coffee or food to wake them up, so even Jamie didn't respond to Massoni. They just nodded and Smith turned to Jamie. "Make sense?"

"Works for me, sir. Let's mount up. Honestly, it will be easier to travel before the snow starts to melt and turns the trail to gunk."

Sue had been successful at the one hour ride up to the Pakistan border to meet NICKLETRUE, but two hours on horseback on the mountain trails was as close to physical torture as she ever wanted to suffer. The prosthetic didn't fit well into the stirrup and she was unable to get a proper seat in the Afghan saddle made of wood, a small bit of leather and one of the fur coats for padding. She was number three of the three 171 riders, so she could squirm and fidget as much as she liked without any unhelpful banter from her team-mates. Every twenty minutes, either Jamie or Wally would come by on a quad-bike to check on the Tomahawks pulling rear security. She sat perfectly still as they went by. As the S&R guys used to say, "Sometimes you just have to embrace the suck."

After two hours in the saddle, all the 171 riders were happy to get off the horses and trade with their mates. Of course, it would take a few minutes for them to get feeling back in their legs and it took longer for Sue to make the necessary adjustments, but after fifteen minutes, she was happy to be walking. She chose a position trailing the other walkers and just in front of her three mounted teammates. This was the standard rotation for nearly twelve hours.

On one of the walking rotations, Sue walked next to Massoni and said, "You notice the Tomahawks only have one quad-bike in the front and one in the rear. The majority of these dudes have been walking all the time. Tough customers, no?"

"Sue, I saw these guys in November '01 going into battle in a sleet storm carrying their weapons and ammo wrapped only in a soaking wet wool blanket. Better yet, they had taken off their boots and laced them around their necks so the boots didn't get wet on the approach march. When they get to the assembly area, they wiped off their feet on the blanket…which by the way doubled as their sleeping bag and raincoat…laced up the boots and fought for six hours. I was in my Gore-Tex and feeling sorry for myself until I saw that hardcore display. These guys are serious, manly men. They may be small in stature, but they definitely have grit." All Sue could do was shake her head. Massoni continued, "Of course, they have been living with war since 1975 and since they are Hazara Shia, they have been living with prejudice for about a thousand years. This is probably too easy for them."

"Jim, when did you become such a philosopher scholar on Afghanistan?"

"I'm just a bundle of surprises. I was an SF medic working with the Klingons when the Soviets were here. I learned plenty then. I happened to be assigned to an SF battalion headquarters when we inserted into Afghanistan and matched up with the OGA pathfinders. As sergeant major, I had time to watch and learn how OGA worked with the Hazara. Haven't forgotten much. Pretty good for a geezer, no?"

At that point, Jamie rode by on a quad-bike and said, "We have about two hours before it gets pitch dark. We need to push for another hour and we should be in the valley. I'm going to tell the Tomahawks to pick up the pace. Massoni, you think you can hang?"

"Jamie, I notice you haven't been doing much walking today. Is that because you are old and fat or because you are a Klingon now?"

"Jim, anytime you want me to carry you, just let me know." With a laugh, Jamie goosed the quad-bike, did a bit of a slide on the trail and headed for the lead Tomahawks.

The morning was a mix of discomfort and glory. Sue rolled out of the sleeping bag and pulled the top cover of the sheepskin robe away from her with a crackle from the light snow that had fallen in the valley overnight. The sky was turning from deep blue to a mix of blue with a horizon of amber. She looked at her watch. 0450hrs. The River Pech was a hundred meters away and roaring from the winter snows that were thawing to the far north. They had built their camp on the second tier of the flood plain which was made up of river tumbled rocks. Not exactly air mattress comfortable, but once they had dug shallow, lozenge shaped holes to get down to the smaller pebbles, it was tolerable. They had made camp in the dark, so this was the first time Sue had a chance to appreciate the deep-sided valley cut by the River Pech. Now that she could see the trail they came down last night, she wondered how in the world they survived the steep descent of the last mile.

Jamie walked past carrying two tin cups of steaming tea. "Good morning, sunshine. I brought you some tea since you seem to be the first one to wake up this bright morning. I would have given the mug to anyone who was awake and you won the prize."

Sue sat up, slowly leveraged herself up onto her feet. She heard her vertebrae pop as she stretched to her full height. "Kinda' cold last night, no?"

"Would'a been warmer if you had put the wool side of the robe against your bag and the skin side out. Creates a better air gap between the bag and the robe."

"And you didn't tell me, why?"

"I figured it would make you wake up early and I would have someone to talk to other than Massoni."

"He's up?"

"He pulled last shift on security with the Tomahawks, so he got up around 0300hrs. Complained all morning when I brought him tea instead of coffee. Like I'm supposed to load a small espresso maker on the horses. Its tea or nothing out here in the Konar."

"Well, I'm grateful for the hot tea. Where do I go to pee right now? All I can see is a circle of Tomahawks, horses, and a few furry lumps that are clearly my pals."

"Sue, you know the drill. Walk in any direction for twenty-five meters out from the perimeter and do the needful. If you head west, you will step down from this bench to the flood plain and the river. It will give you some privacy. Sorta, kinda."

"Twenty five meters is decent. Got it." Sue took her tea and a small kit that carried her toilet gear, strapped on her drop holster with her Glock and headed toward the river. In less than twenty meters, she had dropped below the campsite and nearer to the river. The noise and the water spray reminded her to stay clear of the river's edge. It was not a gentle stream. As Sue walked back toward the campsite, she passed Flash who looked somewhat worse for wear. Her short black haircut was standing on end and she had what could only be described as "pebble face" on her right cheek. Now that Sue had one cup of tea down her throat, she felt almost human, so she greeted Flash, "Nice look, Flash. You work on it all night?"

Flash mumbled, "Coffee. Where is the coffee?"

"No coffee for you. Just tea."

"Bring me caffeine. Any type of caffeine. Soon. Need caffeine. Please."

"Got it. Let me see what I can do." Sue watched Flash stumble as she headed toward the river. As Flash tumbled over the brink and landed face first into the river bank, Sue added with a laugh, "And watch your step."

Flash had recovered and had rolled into a sitting position on the river side. "Leave me alone until you bring me caffeine."

"Yes, ma'am."

By 0600hrs, everyone was on their feet, drinking tea and silently captured by the grandeur of the canyon as night turned into morning. Pluto said, "I always thought the drawings of the 19th century Afghan campaigns exaggerated what they called "the narrow defiles" of Afghanistan. Now I realize it really is like the description and it is a smugglers' paradise."

Wally recognized he had found a fellow romantic and said, "That's why the Brits used "flying columns" of cavalry in the 19th Century. It was the only way to chase the tribals into these valleys and then they used "mountain guns" – cannons that could be carried by mules – to blast them out of their holes in the rock. Today we use UAVs, but in a valley this narrow, you don't get any visibility to use the eye in the sky."

"Good thing, too. Otherwise, I would be out of a job." Jamie said as he walked past the two. "Time to get moving folks. We have about five hours of travel time to get to the safehouse. Sooner would be better than later, ya think?"

Smith nodded to Jamie and turned to his team. "Pack the kit. Tie it down tight since we don't want to sound like a caravan of nomads coming into town."

Massoni started working with each of the team members to ensure that everything was cleared from the campsite and loaded on the horses. As the Tomahawks took the lead and the Americans followed, Pigpen stayed behind to do a double check of the site. Once completed, he broke into a jog to catch up. By the time he reached the column, they were already traveling at their "march pace" that would be set for the rest of the day.

Sue and Flash had both decided to walk rather than ride. The thought of another few hours in the Afghan saddle was too much for them. Pigpen agreed and matched up with his horse that Flash was leading by the bridle. Only Massoni and Pluto were on horseback. Sue said, "You have to figure that sometime during Sergeant Major Academy they remove all the pain receptors from young sergeants major."

"I heard that." Massoni said to no one in particular.

"And they give them enhanced hearing at the same time." Pigpen added.

"And calibrated eyeballs. I lived in fear of my Sergeant Major when I was working in Tampa," was all Flash could add. She was carrying the Remington across her back with a range finder. The bag with extra ammo and her computer was attached to the carpet that served as the saddle for her horse. The rifle ran across her back and extended on both sides of her slim frame with the butt of the rifle only a foot above the ground.

"Right and proper to fear Sergeants Major. Right and proper," was all Pluto said in his raspy squeak of a voice as he rode next to Massoni.

Jameson woke up with the sunrise. He was not entirely used to living in his "gilded cage" in Asadabad, but after what Beroslav told him the previous day, he decided to accept his story until it was proven a lie. Certainly the way he was being treated argued that he was an enforced guest rather than strictly a prisoner. Either way, he decided to start his day properly. He conducted his morning field exercises which were a mix of yoga, tai chi, and basic Army exercises of pushups, situps and squat thrusts. After fifteen minutes, he was ready for a washup in the basin in the bathroom and a change of clothes. Beroslav's team had washed his field kit and delivered it, along with his boots yesterday, so he changed out of the sweats and into clean field clothes. He noticed that the team had done a careful examination of his dive watch and all the seams and pockets of his clothes. They eliminated all of his E&E kit including the wire saw, two button compasses and the two ceramic blades under the sports inserts in his boots. They even found the small ceramic blades secreted in his collar. What he wondered about was why they didn't check his boot heels for concealments. It would appear that the GPS tracker was untouched. Undiscovered? It seemed unlikely given the thoroughness of the search. The fact that they left it in place provided some proof that Beroslav's story had some credibility. Only some, but still enough to make it worth playing out for the near term.

There was a light rap on the door at exactly 0700hrs. Two of Beroslav's men came in with a folding table, another chair and a breakfast tray set for two. Once delivered, they went back into the hallway and Beroslav entered. "We have a busy day and I wanted to have a working breakfast with you. I need to explain what we are doing, where we are going and once again underscore why we are doing this. In the meantime, let us eat." He pulled the cover off the plates to reveal a breakfast of scrambled eggs, chicken kebab meat with tomatoes and onions, and a piece of Afghan bread. Beroslav smiled and said, "No skewer for you to use on me. I don't trust you, yet." He pulled the tea cozy off the tea pot and poured the sweetened, milky Afghan tea into two cups. "I know you served with the British at some point, so you understand the saying *If there is tea, there is hope.* The Afghans say *If there is tea, there is no war.* We Russians say *Drink tea and forget sadness.* I hope these are all applicable today, but at least for now, we can have a decent meal."

Jameson was completely confused by this Russian. He was a smuggler, a former Russian Special Operator, a man who tried to kill Sue O'Connell and yet here he had been nothing but a kind host. Jameson shook his head as he started in on his breakfast as Beroslav outlined the plan for the day.

***

The team arrived at the safehouse on the outskirts of Asadabad by mid-day. The house was actually a walled compound manned by more of Jamie and Wally's Tomahawks. The arrival generated a small celebration as the safehouse team of Tomahawks greeted teammates they hadn't seen since training. Jamie and Wally were treated like tribal elders the safehouse team greeting them with bear hugs and obligatory tea. While the festivities were going on with the OGA, the 171 team moved into the main building and unpacked their kit. Pluto and Flash did little more than drop their rucksacks before they set up the satellite link and plugged in their laptops to get whatever intelligence they could from SOF headquarters in Bagram. Sue had learned her lesson and decided not to annoy her partners while they opened communications. She diligently unpacked her ruck and did the same for Flash's ruck. It wasn't much, but it was the least she could do for her. Pigpen was next door doing the same for his ruck and Pluto's ruck. Smith and Massoni were in the room closest to the stairwell.

Ten minutes later, Sue arrived next to Flash with a cup of Massoni's "sergeant major coffee" for Flash and one for Pluto. "An offering to the brain trust," was all she said.

"And about time too! This is thirsty work," was all Flash could offer. Pluto just nodded as he had already taken the white ceramic mug and was pushing the black coffee down his throat.

Smith and Massoni arrived and offered coffee mugs to Pigpen and Sue. Smith said, "I checked with Jamie and Wally. They have local work to do so we need to get started without them. Pluto and Flash, make us smarter!"

Pluto took the lead in the briefing. His squeaky whisper forced everyone to move closer to him as he explained what they now knew. "We have set up a live feed with the UAV over Asadabad. Just as we did with the Mohmand operation, there will be one bird always on call. The latest from the bird is that Jameson's GPS is in a compound on the East side of town, straight line distance about 2 klicks away from here. Of course, there are no straight roads in Asadabad, so we are looking at about a twenty-minute ride by car. The targeted coverage from the Fort has picked up a number of very different feeds. Apparently, there were several parties ready to pay for Jameson and they were angry that the Russian beat them to the auction. There are at least two different outfits trying to find the Russian and Jameson. One from al Qaida with links to the Haqqani network and one from the Pakistani Taliban who were super pissed that the Russian got away and killed Din Mohammed with booby trapped funds. They did mention that the Russian might have had a team with him because they found a bunch of dead guys at Din Mohammed's compound."

"It's not our fault. Well, not completely," was all Flash had to say.

Smith gave Flash a stern look and she went back to work on her computer.

Pluto continued, "What is a little troubling is the UAV feed includes a couple of new SUVs arriving in the target compound about an hour ago. No telling what that means since there was no cell or satcom calls from the area.

Flash took over at this point, "Our boys in J-Bad have set up a meeting right at 1845hrs for 375 in Asadabad. They sent a map for the car pickup point. I'm hoping Jamie has a car we can use because I'm thinking the horses aren't going to work all that well at a car pickup site."

Smith turned to Flash, "What's the news on Joe?"

"Apparently out of the hospital, desk bound but working in J-Bad and driving everyone crazy, especially Adam." Sue felt particularly embarrassed by this exchange. She had been so focused on Bill Jameson she had completely forgotten her 171 colleague Joe had been in an ambush in Tor Kham the same time that Jameson was kidnapped. She wasn't surprised that Smith and Massoni were able to focus on multiple issues at the same time, but at this point in her career, she should have been at least a bit interested in one injured colleague while still able to worry about another.

Smith turned to Sue and Pigpen. "OK. Get the map, get a vehicle, go to the meeting with 375. If I recall, he is a decent English speaker, so Pigpen, you will be primary. Sue, if there is any difficulty, you will be backup and use your Dari. Don't forget, we are in bad guy country still, so I want both of you to have your heads on swivels so you don't end up in an ambush."

"Check, Boss" they said in unison.

Flash had linked her laptop to a printer she found in the safehouse. She printed out a brief summary of 375, contact information including Adam's bona fides they would use to get the agent to agree to get in the car, and a map of the car pickup location. She handed them the material and said, "This is why you guys are here, so don't mess it up."

Massoni walked by on his way to the coffee pot, "That's my line, Flash. So…you two, what she said."

"Roger, Jim," was all Sue said as she walked out the door to look for Jamie or Wally to sort out transportation. They had two hours before the meeting and that wouldn't be much time to study the material and get out on the street. Pigpen looked at the brief and then walked over to Pluto to get what they all knew was the rest of the story – what 375 was really like.

Pluto said, "He has been a good asset. He doesn't ask for much other than his regular pay. He doesn't seem to embellish and he knows his town. If there is any information out there on the street, he should be able to deliver. Just remember, 375 is a Tajik living in a Pashtun town. He is working for us because he thinks he is smarter, better educated and far more noble than any Pashtun that he might meet. The first two prejudices are reasonable since he was well on the way to a medical degree when the Taliban took over in the early 90s and assumed education was a sign of either weakness or lack of piety. As to nobility, well, 375 has a pretty big ego, so that part of the story is still up for grabs. He speaks fluent Dari and Russian and has reasonable English. That's it." Pigpen nodded, thanked Pluto and headed out of the TOC to find Sue.

Jamie looked hurt when Sue asked him if he had a vehicle at the safehouse. "Really, Sue. You think we are complete idiots? Yes, we have vehicles and they actually run. Puhlease. Next question."

"Can we use one tonight?" Sue tried her most girly-girl smile.

"That's stuff doesn't work on me, kid. Well, not usually. There was this time with Flash..." Before Sue could push that story, Jamie nodded and turned toward what was originally a stable inside the compound. They opened the wooden door and turned on a light. Two vehicles were covered in gray nylon.

"Keeps the owl shit off the vehicle. I hate cleaning owl shit when I am in a hurry."

"Which we are, so which one do I get to take?"

"How about we take both out tonight. I know the streets here and while I'm sure you SOF folks know everything about everything, I would feel better if I was in trail making sure you didn't end up some-place you shouldn't. I might even offer to take Massoni for a joy ride. What'dya think?"

"OK, by me. Pigpen and I will be holding the meeting. You got something that will allow him to sit in the back with 375 while I drive?"

Jamie walked over to the first vehicle and said, "Voila!" as if he was a carnival magician. As he pulled off the nylon, Sue saw what she was convinced was the world's smallest mini-bus.

It was some sort of Japanese tradesman's van, painted flat black with multiple sets of driving lights on the front and "blinders" on the rear. It was only five feet wide and seven feet long. "Cool, huh?" It was left hand drive, a plus in Afghanistan and an automatic which was a plus for Sue since she hated working a clutch with her prosthetic. It was tiny, but there was room in the back for two men, barely. "Pigpen is gonna love this."

"Excellent. The keys are in the ignition. Turn it over and pull it out. I will get my vehicle out next." He walked back and pulled the nylon cover off an ancient military vehicle with a canvas top and canvas doors. Sue looked twice and realized it was a World War II Jeep.

"Where in the world did that come from?"

"Lend Lease to the Brits or maybe the Soviets or maybe the Iranians. Beats me. I found it in a mechanics shop along with a Russian courier bike with sidecar. The Jeep still had the U.S. Navy shipping invoice for delivery to Bandar Abbas harbor. The courier bike still had the instruction manual – all in Russian. I paid a little more and got the Soviet PKM machine gun that attached to the gun mount on the sidecar. I suspect Jim and I might look a little suspicious using that tonight."

"Ya think?"

"Get your vehicle out of the way and I'll get the Jeep ready. What time you reckon you need to depart?"

"Looks like the CPU is about two miles away on the South end of the city. I reckon we leave in an hour, find a layup site and roll into the CPU on time."

"Wrong answer, kiddo. We don't layup here. If you stop, you get covered in visitors, some not so pleasant. You must remember that from J-Bad and I suspect we learned how unpleasant that can be from Bill Jameson's experience. We just roll and I recommend we roll more or less straight outta here to the CPU. I will be following you and can pull countersurveillance. So, we have about 90 minutes."

"You know the town."

"Sadly, I do."

A little over an hour later, they drove out of the compound and headed into the city. Sue was driving the "micro-van" as they decided to call it with Pigpen folded into the back seat providing turn by turn directions. They were both linked by Jamie's communications system to his vehicle. He promised they would stay on course and on time. Massoni decided to ride with Jamie. Flash had volunteered, but Massoni told her to forget it, he was riding with his old buddy. They were sufficiently "gunned up" that if Sue and Pigpen had any trouble, they were certain Jamie Shenk and Jim Massoni would ride to the rescue. That was demonstrated when Sue noticed Jim load an RPG launcher and three rounds for the launcher into the Jeep.

"Expecting a T-62 tank?"

"Sue, you never know. What I do know is the sound of an RPG headed in your direction is one of those visceral sounds that make you want to run away. Any bad guys you might meet won't be able to stand still if they hear a round sent in their direction. I promise."

Massoni's comments reminded Sue of her first tour in Jalalabad with S&R. It was just after US forces had fought in the Black Mountains of Tora Bora. The team was surveilling a support agent for what the analysts insisted was part of an Al Qaida cell in the mountains. They followed him east out of the city and were on the main highway headed toward the Pakistan border when he went around a bend in the road and they drove directly into an ambush. The team knew it was an ambush when five RPG rounds headed their way all at once sounding like rocket propelled freight trains. The good news was the ambushers couldn't shoot for shit so the rounds exploded 100 meters past them in farm fields on both sides of the road. The bad news was by the time they had deployed out of their vehicles and set up suppressive fire, their target was gone as were the ambushers. When they finally stood at the place where the ambushers shot the RPGs, all Jameson could say was "They definitely went to bad-guy shooting school. No one should have missed from this location."

There were no such problems that night as the pair of vehicles headed into the darkness on the edge of Asadabad. The drive into the city was uneventful other than the usual madness of cargo trucks, cars, vans, camels, oxcarts, horse carts, and pedestrians trying to occupy the same place at the same time. It had been years since Sue had to handle a street in Central Asia. Despite the cold sinking into Asadabad from the mountains as the twilight turned into night, she found herself sweating from white-knuckle driving. Sue pulled the van up to the CPU just as the vehicle clock turned 1842hrs. "Not bad given I never drove the route before," she thought. Waiting on the side of the road was a lonely figure captured in the small headlights of Jamie's micro-bus. 375 was a 43-year-old Tajik who now worked as a garbage man and house cleaner in the town. Years of hard, stoop labor had crippled his body and he looked about 70.

Sue pulled up and Pigpen opened the sliding side door and greeted 375 with the parole they received from Adam. "Sir, we are lost and need to know the way to Jalalabad." 375 nodded and climbed into the van.

"Captain Joe told me you would be here. What is your name?"

"I am the Captain's lieutenant. My name is Peter." Pigpen offered his hand and 375 offered his gnarled, scarred hand in return.

Sue watched the exchange through the rear view mirror. She had never teamed up with another 171 handler before and she was interested to see how Pigpen was going to handle the session. Pigpen's debriefing would be broadcast to Jamie and Jim in their vehicle and back to the TOC at the safe house.

"Sir, I apologize for the emergency call, but we need your help more than ever. One of our men, a brother soldier of both the Captain and I has been kidnapped. We need to find him. Please help."

375 nodded so vigorously and so deeply that at one point, Sue thought he had fallen off the seat. "Mr. Peter, everyone knows of your trouble."

"Everyone?"

"The kidnap of a soldier by Din Mohammed has been the talk for days. Then a group of Shuravi took him from Din Mohammed and killed the Mohmand leader." More nodding.

Sue could see in the mirror Pigpen was puzzled. She keyed her microphone and whispered, *"Soviets or Russians, brother."* Her voice communications fed into both Pigpen's earpiece and into the earpieces of Jamie and Jim Massoni. She just didn't want Pigpen to start asking questions that would only delay the necessary debriefing. Pigpen nodded in the mirror and then his eyes nearly bugged out of his head. Sue looked up to see she was driving the van dangerously close to the south end of a camel going north. Another second and they would be goosing the camel that was overloaded with boxes of cargo. In the darkness, Sue was certain that on top of the load was a baby camel looking down at her. She braked, hard, which disrupted the debriefing in the back and generated a comment from Massoni.

"Let's just focus on the driving, O'Connell and let Pigpen to the debriefing. OK?" Sue used her microphone switch to send RR in morse code meaning "Roger, Roger."

The debriefing continued in the back. "We all heard the story and I knew you would call. The Shuravi took him to a house on the East side of the city."

Pigpen asked quickly, "Can you show us the place?"

"Why not?" More nodding from 375. Sue focused on her driving so she could reverse course if she had to. "It is close to here." He started to give directions that, more or less, made sense to her, especially after Jamie offered some local knowledge.

After ten minutes of twists and turns, they approached the compound which looked like every other compound on the street. High brick walls, a steel gate large enough to accept a cargo truck and little else visible from the street. It reminded Sue of the S&R safe house in Jalalabad that served as her home for nearly two years. Memories of her S&R team, Jameson, Massoni and Max Creeter flooded into her mind along with the adrenaline rush from her memory of the gunfight in the alley where she lost her leg. Her thoughts returned to the present when she heard 375 say "That is where they kept him."

Like many handlers used to working with assets in a language where either the case officer or the agent were not fluent, Pigpen immediately caught the use of past tense. "Where they kept him or where they keep him."

More nodding from 375. "Where they kept him. They left today."

Through the radio, Sue heard Pluto's squeaky voice from the TOC say, *"Sweet mother of God."* The emotion flooded across the radio network.

Pigpen remained focused. "Do you know where they took him?"

"Who?"

Sue was prepared to reach back and choke 375, but nearly two years working in the Horn of Africa with tribal leaders, mercenaries, and pirates made Pigpen more patient. "My brother, sir. My brother."

375 only nodded once in response. This time from side to side. "I do not know." Pigpen could see Sue's shoulders collapse in the driver's seat in front of him.

"Can you help us?"

"I have this sealed note. It was left at the compound. My cousin who cleans the compound. He gave it to me. I do not know. I cannot read English. My school only taught Dari and Russian." He handed the note to Pigpen. In a clear printed style, the note was addressed to SUSAN O'CONNELL.

Pigpen did the nodding this time in Sue's mirror. "Thank you so much my brother. You are a true friend. You may have saved my friend's life."

"Inshallah." Was all 375 said.

They dropped off the Tajik a half mile from the pickup site. Pigpen handed 375 a small, heavy wrapped parcel before he left. 375 disappeared into the darkness as Sue pulled away.

As soon as they reported him clear of the vehicle, Smith asked on the radio, *"Did he take the gold?"*

"Yes, sir."

"He deserved it."

"Yes, sir. To think this guy was going to be a doctor some day and now years of physical labor have changed his hands into claws."

Jamie chimed in, *"There is a reason why everyone hates the Taliban. Even the new Taliban hate the old Taliban…mostly."*

"What was in the envelope?" was all Sue said on the net as they pulled away and toward the safe house.

"Don't know. It's addressed to you."

"Unbelievable" Flash said over the radio.

───────────────────────────

Sue nearly killed a half-dozen pedestrians, two donkeys and another mini-van driver in her rush to return to the Asadabad safe-house. After the near miss with the mini-van, Pigpen reached over the front seats and grabbed Sue by the back of the neck. He squeezed hard. "If you intend to kill yourself, that's fine by me. Just let me out of the van now and I'll catch a ride back to the safehouse with Jamie and Jim." The comment was just barely enough to get her to slow down and follow the return route at a reasonable pace without killing anyone.

As they pulled into the compound, Pigpen dismounted from the back of the van in what could only be called a huff. He walked over to the jeep with Jamie and Jim Massoni and leaned into the passenger side door and started talking to the two senior operators. Sue unbuckled her seat belt and marched into the safehouse, slamming the door behind her. She walked through the TOC, up the stairs, and into her sleeping quarters and slammed the door. Pluto and Wally watched the entire "O'Connell storm surge." Pluto said in his whisper voice, "What was that all about?"

Flash put her hand on Pluto's shoulder as she got up. "Let me find out."

Smith stood up and raised his hand. "Flash, right now we need to find out what Taylor found out in the meeting. Let O'Connell chill a bit. If she gets her shit back together, then we are good. If not, nothing you can say will help. OK?"

Flash nodded and responded, "Yes, boss."

Pigpen, Jim, and Jamie entered the TOC and went directly to the coffee pot and poured themselves a cup.

Smith looked at Pigpen and started the debriefing, "So, what do you know that I didn't hear on the radio?"

"Other than the fact that O'Connell has lost her mind?"

"Yes, other than that, Taylor." Smith sometimes used their first names and sometimes used their last names and the entire 171 team accepted the fact that last names meant "be serious." Pigpen got the message loud and clear.

"I reckon you figured out Jameson is no longer in Asadabad. 375 was pretty clear about that. At least, as clear as he seemed to be throughout the debriefing, which means, not super clear."

"We got something written from him, correct? Let's see it."

"It's addressed to Sue."

"It is part of the operation. I doubt it is fan mail." Smith held out his hand and Pigpen passed the letter over to his boss. Smith used his clip knife to open the envelope and pulled out three sheets of paper. Two were in carefully printed writing; the third was a map of an area in Pakistan. Smith put the three sheets of paper down on the large work table in front of him. He figured he could either read the letter out loud with everyone on the team looking over his shoulder or place the letter on the table so they could all read it at once. They read the letter.

Ms. O'Connell and to her teammates,

As you realize at this point, my name is Nicolai Vladimir Beroslav. I am the son and grandson of members of the Soviet Special Services. I currently have Chief Warrant Officer William Jameson under my protection. I am interested in providing Mr. Jameson to you in exchange for you accepting me as a defector.

Given my background and my most recent role as a smuggler of sophisticated weapons to both the Afghan Taliban and the Iraqi Shia militias, I believe I can be of some value. You may wonder why I would do this. I wish to have my revenge against the Russian special services who killed my family in Istanbul. When they killed my family, they ended any loyalty that I might have had to the oligarchs and the Russian government. Up to that point, my work was entirely sanctioned and supported by the Russian government and I can provide specific names, dates and places where I met with my government contacts. Further, I can provide you with compromising information that might be of use in future recruitment operations among my former colleagues.

If you are interested in this offer, please meet me inside the Buddhist mon-

astery in Takht Bhai as soon as you can get there. Please note, there is some urgency because I believe both the Russian Special Services and the Taliban intend to execute both Mr. Jameson and myself if they can capture us. That is why we are leaving Afghanistan and moving to the Swat Valley. It is relatively peaceful there and should be a good place to meet.

Yours very sincerely,

NVB

"No, no, no! Do not trust him. He is absolutely our enemy." Sue had walked into the room and read the note after everyone had finished.

"O'Connell, sit down and let's talk this through."

"No need for talk. We need to get a raid team in there, save the Chief and kill Beroslav. Better still, we intercept them on their way to this monastery and do the needful with long guns and save Bill."

Massoni carefully touched Sue on the right elbow. She shrugged his touch but looked at him, which was why he touched her. Massoni quietly said, "Sue, you need to sit down, be polite to the Colonel and the rest of us, and work as part of a team. If you don't want to be part of the team, that's fine. I just think you need to rejoin the team. Or," Massoni looked her in the eyes and put an edge on his voice, "You can play no part in this operation and when we are done and home, you can RTU." Massoni smiled his most scary Command Sergeant Major smile and closed with, "Whatdya think, O'Connell?"

The threat of RTU – returned to a conventional unit – hit Sue like a punch in the nose. While she had seen Massoni and others threaten SOF operators with the most embarrassing of career changes, no one had ever threatened her with RTU before this. For the first time, she realized the power of being shunned by her SOF family. It was a threat of exile. The SOF community would know she had been sent away. The conventional community would welcome her back but even there everyone would know that she was exiled because of some grave misdeed. No one in the Army would ever trust her again. Massoni's short speech forced her to face the fact that she had taken a very large step outside the bounds of SOF tribal rules. She took a deep breath, looked around the room and said, "Sorry, teammates. I wasn't thinking straight."

Smith hadn't decided yet if he was going to accept the apology or not, but he nodded and said, "No worries, Sue. It's good to have some passion, so long as it is tempered by a willingness to work with the team."

Pluto leaned up to Flash and whispered, "If that is just passion, I would hate to see O'Connell when she is angry." Flash elbowed Pluto in the ribs, hard.

Smith invited everyone to the table as he picked up the three sheets of paper, folded them carefully and put them in a side cargo pocket in his trousers. He knew that the best possible solution for this problem was going to come out of this team, but he also knew that he needed to manage the discussion so that everyone could offer thoughts without interruption. He started with the easy question as he looked at Wally and Jaime. "You guys able to go that deep across the border into Pakistan without asking permission?"

For a change, Wally spoke for them both. "Colonel, you know the border is a pretty difficult thing to identify up here in the mountains. Sometimes even the GPS doesn't work well enough to know for sure where Afghanistan ends and Pakistan begins. Also, I know a bit about the Buddhist monasteries in the region. Lots of them look alike. You could mistake an Afghan ruin for a Pakistani ruin."

"Real easy to mistake," was all Jamie said.

"Especially if the Tomahawks are our guides." Wally concluded.

"It is a challenge, no doubt," Smith said, then asked "If you made that mistake, there could be consequences. You know that right?"

Wally and Jamie nodded and Jamie said, "We're in for the full run, Colonel."

Smith then turned to Pluto and Flash and said, "What do we know from the UAV and from the Fort?"

Pluto started the intelligence briefing, "Bagram reported that they picked up Jameson's GPS tracker moving toward the Pakistan border. The route is consistent with a route that would take them to Takht Bhai. The Fort provided us with some material suggesting the

Haqqani network and some al Qaida folks were hunting for Jameson and his Russian captor on the Afghanistan side of the border. They are determined to get their hands on a US soldier and do the video execution routine." At that point, Flash actually punched Pluto in the side. "What?" was all he said.

Massoni said, "We all know that version of the endgame, Pluto."

Flash took over, "There is something else that supports the letter, Boss."

"Go ahead."

"The UAV bird we have tasked has some tactical sensors onboard and the sensor package includes an intercept capability. It appears that Beroslav and Jameson are also being hunted by Russian speakers. A summary of the text makes it sound like they are more interested in Beroslav than Jameson, but they intend to find, fix and finish both of them wherever they are. These guys are using commercial encryption. Possibly Russia mercenaries? PMCs?"

Jamie added, "Russian private military contractors have been identified in our turf. We haven't been able to figure out why since they aren't exactly friendly with either the Taliban or AQ."

Pigpen added, "I saw the same thing in Africa. They are ready and willing to run guns to anyone so long as there is a profit. We tracked Russian PMCs into Somalia for goodness sake supporting just about anyone who would pay the price. Piracy generated the dough and oligarch juice gave them access to plenty of small arms."

Pluto continued, "If Beroslav was running guns, he probably wasn't running them on his own. Maybe the PMCs were the muscle for the gun-running operation."

Sue finally had something to add, "That's consistent with the outfit that Beroslav was running with when he was in Cyprus."

Smith decided to focus the conversation and said, "Is there anything that suggests our competitors know where Beroslav and Jameson are or where they intend to go?"

Pluto shook his head and said, "Not that I can see."

"So, we have a head start on them."

"By a little," Massoni added.

Jamie smiled, "A little might be enough if we get started soonest.

The Tomahawks have used a route that gets them across the border to the south end of the Swat Valley in three hours and change. Great place to hunt terrorists doing cross-border attacks against our guys here in the Konar or, so I've heard."

Smith looked around the table and ended by looking at Sue. "O'Connell?"

"Boss, I'm ready to work as part of the team. I can't say I trust anything Beroslav has said or done, but there doesn't seem to be any good way to sort this out."

Jamie decided to intervene in what he could see was the beginning of a family feud, "Remember your classes at the Farm, Sue. They always said the perfect is the enemy of the good. We don't have perfect, but I think we have good enough and that's all we are going to get."

The informal meeting was finished, some degree of consensus was established, and Smith knew that it was time to move. "Pluto and Flash, see if you can get us any imagery of the Takht Bhai monastery. Do not task any military sources, I just want an open source set of photos. Tourist photos. If the UAV is still following the vehicles, we will get the military grade photos later." He turned to Wally and Jamie. "We need vehicles for the entire team and most of our equipment plus any Tomahawks you think would be willing to go. I need these vehicles to look just like any of the other trucks taking that smuggler's route you are talking about so that we don't draw the attention of the Pakistanis or, for that matter, one of our armed UAVs that might want to take a shot at gun runners."

Pluto squeaked, "Definitely want to avoid that." Flash decided the elbow in the ribs method wasn't working so she gently dope slapped Pluto on the back of his shaved head. "Ow! What was that for?"

Massoni assumed his role as Sergeant Major for the team. He looked at his 1960s military issue watch with a tritium dial. "If we are going to get to Takht Bhai by dawn, we need to be out of here in the next 90 minutes. Flash and Pluto, take down our communications and pull the crypto cards. Leave half of the equipment in Jamie's vault. Keep the laptops and the satcom rig on power to keep a full charge to the last minute." He looked over at Pigpen and Sue, "If you two can get along for the next 90 minutes, I need you to do a complete functions check on all the weapons we are taking with us. Also, figure out the load plan with Jamie so that we are distributed across all the vehicles." He turned to Smith and said, "Boss, anything else?"

Smith turned to the team as they stood up, "This is not going to be easy, but I think we can pull this off if we keep focused and flexible. Beroslav may be a legitimate defector and if he is, he has plenty to talk about to both SOF and to OGA. We need to plan for two contingencies: One, he is leading us into a trap and two, he is on the run and needs to be protected as much as Jameson. Think about this as we are traveling." Smith headed up to his quarters to pack his kit. The team split into groups and headed in different directions in the safehouse.

"Got it, Colonel," was all Jamie said as he headed out the door while Wally started to take down the Agency communications system, and pulled the crypto key. It was on a lanyard and he put it around his neck. He had a small satcom rig already loaded into a separate rucksack, so he spent the time taking the established system apart and putting it into a vault in the safehouse.

KNIGHT'S CROSS
AT THE MONASTERY

T he pair of vehicles travelled the smugglers' trails along the Afghanistan and Pakistan border for most of the evening and into the early morning. Eventually they stopped in a remote clearing on the Pakistan side of the border, ate a cold meal and slept for a few hours until daylight. Jameson and Beroslav were in the first vehicle and four of Beroslav's Chechen mercenaries were in the second. At dawn, they started on a second set of dirt trails that Jameson was fairly certain headed north and slightly east of the city of Peshawar. Throughout the early morning, Beroslav had been relating his story to Jameson. While Jameson had not completely accepted the story – he was after all still handcuffed and shackled by a chain to his seat – he was beginning to understand the purpose of this game of hide and seek. The question remained whether Beroslav was telling him a tale to keep him quiet or a tale to explain what was going to happen. It was simply too soon to tell.

Beroslav had started with his family history. "My grandfather and my father were members of the Soviet Special Services and I simply followed the family way. My grandfather was a member of the KGB counterintelligence unit responsible for eliminating Nazi collabora- tors from both our own patriotic army and the partisans that fought against the Nazis. Peter O'Connell, the grandfather of your colleague, killed my grandfather in France and buried him in the woods. The American OSS and the British SOE were supposed to be allies with the Soviets and certainly hostile to any Nazi collaborators. Yet, they killed him in a forest somewhere in Southern France." He looked at Jameson to see if the American understood. Beroslav wasn't sure and looked back to the road. Jameson noticed Beroslav anticipated the turns well in advance. This was a route Beroslav knew and had chosen for a reason.

Beroslav continued as the two vehicles climbed rocks on a trail which was designed for donkeys and, perhaps, camels, but certainly not a new Toyota Land Cruiser and a Mercedes GLK. "My father joined the KGB First Chief Directorate in the 1960s after his service in the airborne forces. He volunteered to be one of the first officers in the KGB commandos called Alpha Group and was part of the Alpha and Zenith Groups that killed Hafizullah Amin in 1979. You will have read that Spetsnaz did the assault. That is not true. It was the KGB Alpha and Zenith Groups. The Soviet leadership were certain that Amin was going to become another Stalin and was probably one of your assets, only interested in power rather than advancing the political and economic freedom of the Afghan people. He needed to be eliminated. Eventually, you Americans decided to prevent our effort to free the Afghans from their barbarous ways. I suppose now you wonder whether it was worth it."

Jameson had heard this same story in the 1990s when he was in the Balkans with SOF supporting the peacekeeping – actually peace-making – mission. There were Russian paratroopers also in the mix and by that time, the Taliban and al Qaida were working together in Afghanistan. Jameson saw no point in reminding Beroslav that the communist government in Kabul in the 1980s was just as barbarous as the Taliban. The only difference was the ideological justification of the barbarism. On his first tour in Afghanistan in 2002 as an S&R team leader, Jameson heard an Afghan interpreter say "The donkey is still a donkey, they just changed the saddle." The people of Afghan-istan had little optimism when it came to the government in Kabul or in any of their provinces. Jameson just nodded in an effort to keep Beroslav talking. He hoped that somewhere along the way, the story would explain why they were driving to an abandoned Buddhist monastery at the south end of the Swat valley.

"I tried to follow in my father's footsteps. In our housing area in Moscow, I was the youngest member of the party. I joined the Kom-somol and, when I was old enough, I attended the officer academy and fought to be assigned to one of the paratrooper divisions of the USSR. Honestly, the day I was able to wear my sky-blue beret and command a Soviet Desant, sorry, paratrooper force was the best day of my life. My father and mother were very proud. The pride did not last when the Soviet Union collapsed."

Beroslav shook his head and for a moment seemed lost in thought though he may simply have been concentrating on a very steep and dangerous part of the trail. Jameson had noticed the green-faced, Soviet paratrooper field watch on Beroslav's prosthetic wrist. So far, the story matched what Jameson could observe.

"The collapse of the Soviet Union and the breakup of my country killed my father. Literally, he died of a stroke the day Yeltsin stood on a tank and ended the coup that my father was convinced could save our Soviet Union. Shortly after that, my Desant unit was transferred to the new state of Belarus. Great Russians were allowed to leave the unit before the transfer. Based on my father's service, I was accepted into the KGB Alpha Group. And then, the KGB was disbanded. Alpha Group was reassigned to the FSB which was the former Second Chief Directorate of the KGB. I stayed with Alpha Group for nearly five years. Along with the OMON special service troops from the Ministry of Interior, we were the foot soldiers for the protection of the state. In those first years of the Russian Federation, I saw combat outside of Russia in our near abroad, those states who had been part of the Soviet Union. I worked in Georgia, Armenia, Tajikistan, Uzbekistan. Then, I was reassigned inside Russia in Chechnya." Beroslav tapped his prosthetic hand against the steering wheel. "This was my gift for serving the state in those wicked times."

Jameson didn't quite know what to say. He knew of the complete economic and social collapse following the breakup of the Soviet Union. Armed groups fought for control of their newly independent states that had been part of the Soviet Union. Usually, the fighting pitted the former leaders of the socialist republic against ethnic groups long suppressed by the Soviet leadership. In the southern republics, some of those fighting the established state forces were Islamic extremists. Some were simply well-armed gangs. In the case of the Chechen rebels, the fighting generated some of the most dangerous and dedicated supporters of Al Qaida. The Russian fight against them had been brutal and initially a catastrophe for the reputation of Russian combat forces. Eventually, the conflict in Chechnya turned into a scorched-earth replay of Soviet operations at the end of World War II. Artillery and airpower pounded Chechen cities indiscriminately until the rebels surrendered or fled. Everyone caught in the middle died. Those who escaped ended up in either the Ferghana valley in Uzbekistan or in Afghanistan in Usama Bin Laden's foreign fighter battalions. "Brutal," was all he could think to say.

"Brutal barely captures the time," Beroslav continued. "We Russians have been fighting the barbarians in the Caucasus for generations. Tolstoy wrote short stories about their brutality and barbarism. The only difference now is that weapons are more precise and more destructive. In my case, I was wounded by a Russian tank round fired into a building where my team's observation post was located. We were there to identify targets and we ended up targets ourselves because some young, scared tank commander saw movement in the rooftop and fired a main gun round into our building before determining if we were friend or foe. The first round was a direct hit on our position. I was the only survivor and that was only because one of my men was directly in front of me when the round exploded. The tank commander used the second round to collapse the building around us. It was a full day before we were found in the rubble." Beroslav paused again.

"My hand was not the worst of it. The nightmares of being buried alive lasted for years. And then the nightmare of Russia continued. Russia had no money. Russia had a government run by a drunkard and picked apart by US and European business "experts" who only knew how to line their own pockets by lining the pockets of the new Moscow elite. I had no treatment worth speaking about for nearly three months. At the same time, my father's survivor benefits were cancelled. My own benefits were cancelled because I was discharged from service due to my wounds. My mother was thrown out of her apartment to make room for a Yeltsin crony who took over the entire floor of the building as the domicile for his European mistress. My mother nearly died from shock as they moved her out of the apartment that had been her home since 1963. I was in hospital and had no idea until much later how awful Moscow had become. My mother survived and used her connections and my father's connections to be part of the roof for the survivors of this new Russia."

Jameson didn't have any idea what Beroslav was talking about. He thought perhaps the word was some Russian acronym, so he said, "Roof?"

"The oligarchs are neither evil nor good, they just are. Corruption in Russia is just like the weather. Like the Russian winter. Just as everyone needs a roof over their head to protect them from our weather, the syndicates provide protection from the shit that the oligarchs rain down on the people. We ask very little and we give much. We pick and choose which oligarch to support and which to destroy. We work for the people. Sometimes we work for the government, particularly since the arrival of President Putin. He needs people who are loyal to Russia and not necessarily to their pocketbook or to some bureaucracy that has no commitment to the motherland."

Beroslav negotiated a particularly difficult part of the track and then continued, "Some of the syndicates…you call them mafia… were started by Russian Special Services. The KGB leadership in the late 1980s saw the future and moved funds and people to Central Europe just for this contingency. They were the ones who started many of the syndicates. My family connections meant my mother was welcomed into the syndicates."

Beroslav paused and sighed. "I have this sophisticated hand because of the syndicate." He raised his arm to demonstrate the lifelike movement in his prosthetic. "My mother arranged for me to travel to Austria before my arm muscles and nerves atrophied. The syndicate paid for the treatment. Nearly a year in a hospital near Vienna like none that existed in Russia. My loyalty to the syndicate is based on the fact that as my mother started to take more and more responsibility, they provided a roof for my family and many veterans of both wars in Afghanistan and Chechnya."

"A protection syndicate?"

"At first. Then we realized that to do the sort of support we wanted to do for the people, we needed more money. First it was serving as the protectors for selected oligarchs that were loyal to the President. Then, we started smuggling items into Russia for these oligarchs. Guns, cars, whisky, drugs. Whatever the oligarchs wanted for their own use and so long as they paid well."

Beroslav looked Jameson in the eyes. "I know we never smuggled drugs in a volume that would have harmed anyone but the oligarchs. We have an epidemic of drug addiction in Russia. We were not part of that epidemic." Beroslav paused as he negotiated another abrupt turn on the trail. "Finally, we decided to use our smuggling talents in the service of the State. We regularly acquire Western weapons and technology and deliver them to allies of Russia. As you might say, completely off the books."

Jameson took a chance to ask a question that might hit a nerve, "So, how does all of this end up with you trying to kill Sue O'Connell?"

"I grew up with the story of the O'Connell treachery. I hoped one day to be able to kill Peter O'Connell myself. I knew he had been successful in the US special services and had travelled all over the world working against the Soviet Union. I also knew he had lost his wife in suspicious circumstances in Berlin in the early 1960s. Before my time, of course. In those times, no one inside the KGB would have used KGB resources for personal vendettas. That would have been a one-way trip to a gulag, at best. We weren't that far from the Stalin days after all. If she was killed by our special services, there must have been a reason. All I know for sure is it was not a Beroslav who did it. The same thing about O'Connell's son. If I had been the one to hunt him down, I would have put a bullet in his head or a knife in his chest. I knew he was in Tblisi at one point and I tried to arrange a meeting. No luck."

Jameson wasn't certain, but it looked like Beroslav was crying. Not sobbing or sniveling. Just tears running down the slab sides of his face.

"When I heard that the granddaughter of Peter O'Connell was working in Cyprus, in the same country I was working, I thought this is my chance to avenge my grandfather. I suspect you know the story. You probably even know the end of the story when the Russian government decided to kill me on the docks. That I still do not understand. My work in Cyprus was sanctioned, even encouraged, by the government. Why they decided to shoot me instead of rescuing me is still a puzzle. They hadn't planned on me wearing an armor vest with an armored plate front and back. Once I felt the round hit and crack the plates, and enter my back, I had only a second to either fall into the water or stand and take a round in the head. I chose to dive into the water. The weight of the armor did nearly drown me, but I was able to drop the armor and swim along the underside of the dock. I was free."

"There was a time when I thought the GRU was the perpetrator of the attack on me. I found out later it was the Alpha Group from the FSB. They are good shots, but their choice of ammunition was foolish. If they had used the standard, Alpha Group armor piercing bullets, I would have died on that dock in Cyprus."

Beroslav paused and Jameson noted he wiped away a tear that was rolling down his cheek. "Then they decided for reasons I still do not understand, to kill my entire family in Istanbul. We were only conducting operations that were directly approved by the Kremlin. What was the purpose? I heard recently that the same team decided to kill your team in Cyprus. Were they trying to cauterize some open wound? I don't know. All I know now is that I am the last of the Beroslav's and I don't intend to…"

The rifle round hit in the exact center of the Land Cruiser's windscreen as they drove around a left hand turn in the trail. The spider web from the shot went from side to side. The second round shattered the windscreen and pieces fell into Beroslav and Jameson's lap. Given the limitations of the road, Beroslav did an inexact but successful reverse 180 that put the rear of the Land Cruiser in the direction of the shooters. Unfortunately, after the turn, the vehicle jammed against a rock wall with the two right side tires flattened by subsequent shots. Beroslav reached into a vest pocket and threw the handcuff key at Jameson. "Time for you to either trust me or die, Mr. Jameson." Jameson saw Beroslav pull out an AKMS Kalashnikov folding stock assault rifle from the space inside the driver's door.

Beroslav opened the driver's door slightly and began to engage the ridge line were the muzzle flashes continued. The Chechen mercenaries in the trailing vehicle pulled forward and provided blocking cover for Beroslav. Jameson saw the four Chechens roll out from the left side of their Mercedes GLK and take up firing positions. Two had AK74 rifles. One had a PKM belted machine gun and the fourth had a Finnish Valmet bolt action rifle with a military style flash suppressor. All four started to engage the targets on the ridge line as Beroslav reached into the back seat of the Land Cruiser, and shook broken glass from a rifle case. Jameson was now free from his handcuffs and was crawling over the center console of the Land Cruiser and through the open driver's side door.

As Jameson exited the vehicle, Beroslav handed him another AKMS. "I suspect you know how to use this, so please do so," was all Beroslav could say over the chaotic noise of the rounds passing overhead and the returning fire from the Chechens.

Another nightmare drive on smugglers' roads. Jamie had two five-ton, right hand drive cargo trucks decorated in the garish style of Pakistan cargo haulers. The first truck was painted with what were clearly scenes from some Bollywood movie with men on horseback and women dressed in saris and explosions in the background. The second was painted in a scene that could have been from Kashmir or a postcard from Switzerland. Snow-capped mountains, silver-blue lakes and pine trees. Both trucks had small decoratively painted pieces of metal hanging from every horizontal and vertical surface which resulted in the noise that made the US forces in Afghanistan call these haulers "jingle trucks." In the back of the second truck, all Sue could hear was the strain of the diesel engine and the sound falling rocks as they were crushed and tossed aside by a truck on a trail never designed for a vehicle this size. Even with the back canvas open, the ride was definitely as bad as any Sue had in Afghanistan including the infiltration ride into Jalalabad she used in the past. That truck was known as the "vomit comet" but it was nothing compared to this ride. Since they couldn't see what was in front of them, the passengers in the back couldn't brace for the regular left/right/front/back/repeat jolts.

The trucks didn't have the standard long bench seats in the back, so the passengers had to sit on the floor, leaning against the side of the bed with their legs straight out or, as the Tomahawks chose, to sit cross legged. By the time they were across the Afghan-Pakistan border, everyone was covered in dust. In Asadabad, Wally had given each of the 171 team a Pakistan kamiz which was simply a long-tailed wool shirt. He also provided a pakol hat, and a wool shawl which was long enough to hide their weapons. As he passed out his "light disguise," he said, "You aren't going to fool anyone up close, but you might fool someone from a distance. If we meet anyone up close, it's a gunfight anyhow, so it won't matter." Flash couldn't figure out how to wear the pakol, so Sue offered to help. Eventually Flash understood how the hat worked and designed her own, high fashion version of Afghan style. When they had mounted up in the truck, Flash's Afghan hat looked like a cross between a French beret and an illustration in a Dr. Seuss story. By the time they reached Pakistan, her pakol looked like every other pakol in the truck. Crushed and covered in dirt.

It was an hour past dawn when they halted on a mountainside track. Sue realized the only two reasons to stop would be an obstacle or an adversary. Before she could make a decision on which, the Tomahawks leapt out of the truck bed. It looked as if they jumped head first, but Sue could see each one landed on the balls of his feet with his weapon ready for action. Compared to the fighters' ballet-like departure, Sue, Flash and Pluto's dismount was more like a flock of chickens poured out of a crate. Eventually, they got to the front to find a Toyota Land Cruiser jammed against the rock wall, shot full of holes and abandoned. Across the road, there were cartridge cases. Sue noticed right away there was no blood anywhere.

"Looks like someone was ambushed right here and it wasn't more than a couple of hours ago. The engine on the Land Cruiser is still warm to the touch." Wally had already conducted a quick examination of the entire vehicle, inside and out. "There is nothing here. The windshield and the back window are shot out, but no blood. There is a set of handcuffs in the truck, but they are open and the key is still in the cuffs."

Jamie and Massoni were walking around the site. "I see two different types of Soviet cartridges - 7.62mm and 5.54mm, some links to a PKM machine gun and a rifle cartridge in 7.62mm."

"The last cartridge is a Valmet," Massoni said. "Sniper rifle."

"Show off," was all Flash said.

Smith came up to the front. "As interesting as this all is, there are no blood stains here, so whoever was ambushed won the fight. You can see truck tires proceeding down this road. Let's get this trash over the side, so we can get moving."

Jamie spoke a string of instructions in Dari to the Tomahawks and they pushed the Land Cruiser over the edge and down a 200-meter slope into a ravine where it disappeared in a grove of trees and shrubs.

Smith nodded and climbed into the passenger position in the first truck next to Wally. "Mount up. Jamie, can we get the canvas off the front of the bed so that the Tomahawks can engage if necessary?"

"No problem, Colonel." Jamie climbed up the side of the truck, pulled his Randall combat knife out of its belt sheath and sliced the front of the thick canvas like it was paper. He dropped down and did the same with the second truck's canvas. He turned to his Tomahawks and gave them specific instructions. They replied in unison "Chasm" and mounted into the two trucks.

"Chasm?" Flash said.

Pluto replied, "Literally, my eyes. Whatever Jamie order them to do, they responded you can take their eyes if they fail."

"I don't think there is much of a risk of that," Sue said as she climbed aboard with the help of Flash.

The Chechens ended the gunfight quickly and then two climbed up the cliff face to see if there were any shooters left to kill. Once they determined that all of the ambushers were dead, they came down the mountain and informed Beroslav both the results of their counter-ambush response and that they found the ambushers' vehicle on a side trail. Right hand drive Toyota Hi-Lux, Peshawar license plates. It had water and supplies for two nights. There were four ambushers who had rifles and one RPG7 rocket grenade launcher. The Chechens told Beroslav, that the RPG gunner had been killed just as he was loading the launcher. Jameson stayed by the Mercedes with the PKM machine gunner and the Chechen with the Valmet sniper rifle.

Beroslav returned to the vehicle and faced Jameson. "Mr. Jameson, the time has come for you to decide how you want to proceed. My men will go no farther. They need to return to Afghanistan and then on to wherever they choose to go in their dangerous world. We agreed in Asadabad they would take me to the border and then we would part company. They have been well paid in advance and they will receive additional funds as soon as soon as I am able to send and receive messages on my mobile. They are not extremists and they know the longer they stay on the border, the better chance they have of being captured by their fellow countrymen and executed as traitors or being identified as terrorists by your troops and killed. They will take the Mercedes back and we will proceed using the truck left behind by the ambushers. You are armed, you can fight us, or you can proceed with me to Takht Bhai. I have two Russian diplomatic passports with me made out in my name and in a new identity for you, Miroslav Shymkovic. They are relatively good forgeries with the only exception that your photo shows where it was recently added. Still, we should be relatively free from difficulty for the rest of the trip."

Beroslav paused and then continued, "You know my stated plan is to surrender to your team when they arrive. You know I left them a description of where we could meet. You know I didn't destroy your GPS tracker in your boot so even if they didn't get the letter, they know where we are going. If you believe me, then we can proceed together as comrades in arms. If you do not believe me, then you can always kill me along the way. I have crossed the Rubicon, comrade. There is no going back, so either we go forward or I die somewhere between here and some future destination. I know this sounds like a speech and I apologize for this, but I am a Russian and pessimism is in my genes. I need to know now what you intend to do."

Jameson was standing in the middle of the road with his rifle in his hands. He figured he could probably take out one or two of his captors, but not all five of them. He had a weapon, he had time in his favor, his target had just said he was sending his bodyguards back to Afghanistan, and, it just might be Beroslav was telling the truth or, at least, some of the truth. It was not a hard decision. "Nicolai, I'm in. Feel free to call me Bill."

As Beroslav said, they had no difficulties once they were out of the mountains. Beroslav's cover story was they were photojournalists affiliated with *Russia Today* and they were registered with the Russian embassy in Islamabad. He admitted the final part of the story was completely false, but he had bags with cameras, *RT* documentation and even some basic notes on the Khyber and Mohmand tribal areas and the Swat Valley. Jameson could see that this had been a plan for some time, though he figured his role in the plan was new and, most probably ad hoc, once the word got out of his capture.

The transition from the cold of the Afghan mountains to the heat of the valley confluence of the Kabul and Swat Rivers was dramatic. Shortly after they came out of the mountains, they changed out of their sweaters and jackets into shirt sleeves and photojournalist vests. The vests served both to enhance their cover and to hide the fact they were both carrying pistols. As they changed out of their heavy clothes, Beroslav handed Jameson a Makarov pistol in a leather holster. He smiled and said, "It isn't much of a pistol compared to your Glock but it was all I had available. One of the gifts left behind for my Chechens was your Glock; my team leader coveted the weapon and I thought it was only fair. As to the Makarov, I have been told it can't do much damage to a person wearing body armor, but I hope we don't have to find out."

They arrived at the village of Takht Bhai shortly after mid-day. The locals showed no any interest in the two Europeans driving a Toyota Hi-Lux through their villages heading up to the ruins. That said, both Beroslav and Jameson noticed some of the compounds in the area were flying the black flag associated with the Pakistani Taliban known locally at the Tehrik-e-Taliban-Pakistan or TTP.

"Could have picked a site that was slightly less hostile, Nicolai?"

"I could have done so, but I'm not sure I would have been able to avoid the Russian special services and their helpers if we had conducted this meeting in a hotel in Peshawar. People are murdered in Peshawar all the time and no one seems to notice."

"And you think they will notice here?"

"Well, the difference is that we will see them coming."

"Inshallah, Nicolai. Inshallah."

The monastery was on a hillside overlooking the village and the heavily irrigated valley of the Kalpani River. They pulled into what had been a formal, tourist parking lot on the entrance to the sand-colored walled complex. They were greeted by an elderly caretaker who immediately decided they needed a guide. Takht Bhai was one of the UNESCO world heritage sites in the region. Before 9/11 it was visited by foreigners from Islamabad and Peshawar and archeologists from throughout the Western World. Now, it was an abandoned set of ruins that had a single caretaker. Beroslav tried to convince him they did not need a guide. Eventually a substantial bribe freed them from their "guide." Jameson watched as Beroslav handed the man a single coin and whispered in his ear.

"How much did you give him, Nicolai?"

"I gave him a single English gold sovereign from World War II. I found over the years that the only currency of utility is gold and the only gold anyone trusts in Central and South Asia is British gold. It isn't easy to acquire them, but they are very useful when you need them. The ones I have used in the past came from some NKVD operation in the Great Patriotic War. My supply went to the Chechens who rode with us from Asadabad. That sovereign was my last one from a money belt I brought with me over a year ago. As I said when we started this road trip, one way or the other, I won't need them anymore."

"What did you tell him?"

"I told him we were photojournalists and we intended to take many pictures today and tonight and we needed him to keep watch for us to make sure we weren't disturbed. I promised him more when we were done."

"And?"

"Well, I suspect there will be someone carrying money in our rescue party. If not, I will just leave the camera equipment behind. I doubt that pensioner will use the equipment, but he will be able to sell it."

"So, what do we do now?"

"We enjoy the story of Takht Bhai, the only surviving Buddhist monastery in Pakistan and its ties to Alexander the Great. We relax in the shade of the monks' cells and we wait for our rescue or we wait for attackers. This is the end of the road as far as my plan is concerned. If you have another plan, I am ready to follow your instructions."

Jameson looked around the tall brick towers that once held roof timbers for massive buildings on all four sides of the courtyard. Closer to the courtyard were a series of small religious structures that were identified by dilapidated signs as Buddhist stupas. Behind the stupas was a fifty-foot-high wall with dozens of small rooms that had served as the monk's residences. Jameson had been to Thailand when he was on Special Forces training teams and he had toured the great temples of Bangkok. He knew that Buddhism was a religion of statues, brilliant colored flags and draperies and the smell of incense. During his tours in Jalalabad, he had heard from one of the analysts that the Kabul river valley from Jalalabad to the Indus had been all part of a Gandharan kingdom that was captured by Persian Emperors, by Alexander the Great and eventually by the Afghan king, Mahmud of Ghazni. At the time, Jameson listened to this tale that sounded like an adventure novel. Now he was sitting in the middle of a Buddhist monastery just north of the center of this kingdom from over 2000 years ago. All that was left at Takht Bhai were the partially collapsed, brown earth structures as a reminder of a time when this part of the world was not Muslim but linked to a religion that spanned all of China, SE Asia, the Himalayas and the Hindu Kush. The remnants of an outpost older than two millenium captured his imagination for a moment.

He turned away from the ancient and back to Beroslav focusing his attention on his current situation. Jameson had served in many conflicts with many allies and more than his share of adversaries. He had grown up in the Cold War and joined the Army when all the war scenarios had the Red Army as the enemy. The end of the Soviet Union had shifted Army priorities and he had trained for a new conflict against terrorists and non-state actors. In that new role, he had killed men he didn't know and even a few that he did know after following them for weeks at a time. Now, he was standing next to a man who had tried to kill one of his friends, who was at the very least a member of one of the most dangerous criminal enterprises on the planet. And this man had purchased Jameson from kidnappers in hope of purchasing his own freedom from his past. Long ago, Jameson learned to live in the "gray zone" of espionage and treachery. This was a new level of complexity and while he was by no means a slow learner, he was fighting to answer the question: Ally or adversary?

He turned to Beroslav and asked, "Can you make some tea?"

Beroslav reached into the rucksack at his feet and said, "Yes, I just happen to have a small stove, a pot for water and a separate pot for tea."

The tea was Russian and stronger than Jameson liked, but it wasn't as if he had an option. They looked down on the approach to the courtyard and could see twenty miles along the road to the west. This would be where the US team would travel and looking out at that middle distance kept them occupied for a while. Jameson started a conversation that he had been keeping in his head for days. "Nicolai, why go to all this trouble? Why not just…just walk out of the mountains, into a US facility in Afghanistan or Pakistan and ask for asylum?"

In his mind, Beroslav had asked and answered this question many times.

He said, "No. In my business, we all know too much about one another. If any of my…colleagues saw any hint I was planning to leave, they would have made that departure…permanent. When I heard that you were captured and up for sale, I realized this would provide a cover story. I told them I was settling an old score. My colleagues understand vendettas all too well. They wished me well and I left without any trouble."

"But again, once I was in your custody, why not just take me to the closest US base?"

"Because, my friend, even your special operations units are penetrated by the Russian special services. If we walked into a remote base in Afghanistan and your colleagues reported it to your headquarters in Kabul and then Ft. Bragg, you and I would be dead by the next day along with most of the base soldiers. This is a game of cat and mouse and I am hoping that this time, the mouse gets to escape because the cat doesn't know where to look."

Jameson decided that this was about as much as he could expect from Beroslav for the time being. He would have to let the debriefers handle the rest of the story. After another pot of tea, they shared the sort of stories that intelligence officers and special operators regularly trade with both allies and adversaries: Amusing anecdotes that are sufficiently generic that they give away no secrets but focus on successes and failures of "the trade." Jameson was the first to finish his tea. He stood up and said, "We need to continue this conversation, but I have to pee."

"You first and then I will. You have the entire compound to use as your latrine."

As he cleared the entrance of the cell, the wooden rifle butt of an ancient Kalashnikov hit Jameson in the back of the head and sent him tumbling down the scree slope in front of the monk's cell. Beroslav looked up into the faces of a half dozen young men in black shalwar kamiz, black turbans, long hair and long beards. As Beroslav stuggled to get up and reach for his pistol, he received a similar butt strike to the head. Just before he lost consciousness, Beroslav realized they were probably sitting on top of a Pakistani Taliban safehouse. It was not an exaggeration to think that the end result would not be good.

———

Once the trucks completed their descent from the mountains, the ride got smoother if not exactly more comfortable. Midday in March on the plains of the Khyber Agency are hot and dry. The riders in the back of the trucks couldn't shed most of their wool garments for fear of revealing both their nationalities and their armed status. So, they raced along the highway, trying to keep a low profile. The passengers in the back sweated.

Sue turned to Pluto on her left and said, "Any chance you know where we are and how long we are going to have to live in this canvas torture chamber?"

"Eh?" Pluto had been asleep and he woke to see Sue directly in his face. It was terrifying.

Sue said in her slowest, most careful tone, "I said, where are we now?"

Pluto looked out the back of the truck at the irrigated fields and the mountains on the Western horizon. His squeaky whisper barely reached Sue's ear. "Ball park, about 50 kilometers into Khyber Agency. Probably less than another 50 to Takht Bhai."

"Been there?"

"A long time ago as a student. Takht Bhai is the only surviving complete Buddhist monastery in Pakistan. Same folks who built the giant Buddhas in Bamian. Most were destroyed by religious zealots."

"Recently?"

"Only if you measure time in millenia."

Flash was watching the conversation and decided to join, "I don't."

"Me neither," was all Sue could offer.

"Well, Takht Bhai is from before the time of Alexander the Great and his invasion of Asia. There was a Buddhist empire called Gandhara and he conquered it. The subsequent mix of Buddhist and Greek design is known as Gandharan Art. Buddhist icons with Greek flowing robes. The Gandharans…"

"Enough already. I really don't care one way or the other. I just wanted to know when we were going to get there."

Pluto looked hurt. He shook his head and said, "You were the one who asked. One thing you do need to know is that it is a hillside fortress. The remains include walls, towers, a courtyard and about a hundred little rooms for monks."

"So, easy to defend."

"And easy to hide in if you are trying to do so."

"Great."

Pluto didn't pick up on Sue's sarcasm so he continued, "Well, yes, it would be great for hiding."

Flash gave Pluto a "cut throat" sign to end the conversation before Sue decided to punch him. Pluto looked surprised and hurt, but remained silent.

They pulled up to a small village as the sun was just above the western horizon. Smith was using the map that Beroslav included in the message. Beroslav had noted a small track that came around the village and ended at the northern base of the monastery. Smith used the radio link between the two vehicles and said, *"We will be moving through the village and heading on what looks like a tractor route. We need to be careful of the locals. I noticed a fair number of black flags flying over the compounds as we arrived. This isn't Shia country so that means it is the black flag of the Taliban."*

Massoni was in the second vehicle and responded, *"Check, boss. Simple message: Don't run over the kids or the cattle."*

They geared down and headed through the village and out into the fields. The villagers were already inside their compounds with gates closed so if they noticed the noise of the trucks, they certainly didn't open any gates to look out. Too many questions, too few answers, too many villains since 9/11 had made most villages in Pakistan hostile to any outsiders and definitely nervous of visitors.

The map showed an open space at the end of a plowed field and they turned the trucks around there and parked them in a gathering of low scrub trees. While the fields were lush from irrigation from the river, any plant life outside the irrigated fields was colored in multiple shades of brown from dust, too much sun and not enough water. Once the vehicles stopped, the Tomahawks dismounted and set up a defensive perimeter around the trees.

Smith instructed Pluto and Flash to set up the satcom rig and see if they could download any new information. While they were accomplishing that job, Smith brought together the rest of the Americans and sat them down in a circle behind one of the trucks.

"I reckon we can get into the monastery in about twenty minutes when we still have light to do so, but not enough light to show us climbing the hillside. Any thoughts?"

Massoni took charge, "Boss, I recommend we split into two small parties approaching the monastery from slightly different angles. I don't know what we are going to find up there, but I don't want it to be a surprise."

"Agreed. Jamie and Wally, can the Tomahawks help?"

"Colonel, we have just enough Tomahawks to secure the trucks. They would love to be in a fight, but I recommend they stay so our trucks are here when we get back."

"Village thieves?"

"Like something out of Ali Baba would be my description. They probably wouldn't actually take the trucks, but they would take everything they could from the trucks including tires and wheels and canvas. When you are poor, anything extra is a bonus."

"So, no Tomahawks."

"No sir. And either Wally or I have to stay with them to prevent them from raiding the village. I don't know what they would find in the village, but "pillage a village" is what they see as a bit of light-hearted amusement. They see it as better than TV." Jamie smiled his most helpful smile.

Pluto and Flash entered the mix at that point. Pluto started the debriefing. "The latest UAV images show an empty courtyard in the middle of the monastery. Only one vehicle in the area, a Toyota Hi-Lux parked in the tourist parking lot below the monastery. That UAV had to pull from its orbit an hour ago and the next one should be on station in 20 minutes. The new one is armed."

"Good," was all Jamie had to say.

Flash continued, "The UAV captured mobile calls from several groups headed this way. They don't know precisely where the two guys are located and they are starting in the villages around Mardan and then heading North. Pluto says Mardan is close."

"We drove through it a half hour ago just before we turned into the village."

"One final thing, boss. There is a Russian team out here somewhere. The UAV picked up military encrypted voice again and the Bagram geniuses say the encryption is Russian commercial encryption. PMCs most likely since the Russian government encryption is far more serious. Still, the Bagram folks haven't had any success with the decrypt and have pushed the material to the Fort."

"Great. So, any alibi rounds before we take off?"

No one spoke, so Smith said, "Massoni, you, Jamie and Taylor take one route. I will take O'Connell and Billings on the other. Pluto, you stay here with Wally and manage the UAV feed. You may need to serve as our fire support from the armed UAV, though I hope we don't have to use Hellfires to get out of here. Wally, you manage the Tomahawks both as our rendezvous point and, God forbid, as our QRF. All clear on your jobs?"

Nods all around. They pulled on rucksacks with ammunition, medical gear and radios and headed up the dirt trails on the Takht Bhai hillside.

Massoni, Jamie and Pigpen reached the walls of the monastery first. The monastery had an exterior wall that ran along the top of the ridge and then a second set of walls that led directly into the monastery ruins. The exterior wall had multiple entry points where the two thousand year old mud bricks had collapsed. The sun was now just below the horizon. They knew they had about a half hour before dark.

Pigpen said, "I wish I had my green eyes with me."

Jamie had taken a knee and was reaching in his ruck. "Never leave home without mine."

"OK, wiseguy, then you lead the way." Massoni pointed toward the closest gap in the wall. Jamie had his night vision goggles on a head harness. They were flipped up for now, but would be flipped down and turned on when needed.

Smith, Sue and Flash reached the top of the ridge and looked at the exterior wall from another vantage point. Smith turned to Flash. "So, Flash. You ready to use your long gun skills again?"

"Count on it, boss."

Smith pointed to where the interior wall had crumbled. "Get up there and set up. Did you bring the night sight as well as the standard optics?"

"Sir, I am hurt you need to ask."

"Then why am I still talking to you? Get going." Flash darted along the wall that would give her visibility to what they hoped was the entire courtyard. Smith watched her disappear into the shadow of a wall and then sent a quick radio message.

"All, 6. Flash in place. We are moving to the courtyard from the west."

"6, 5. We are moving to the courtyard from the north."

"All, Pluto. Bird on station in 4mikes."

"Get started."

The two teams moved quickly over the rubble of the exterior wall and toward areas where they could gain entry to the courtyard. Flash's voice came on the radio, filled with worry: *"All, I have five, no six in the courtyard plus our two. Our two are tied back to back. The six are all dressed in black shalwar kamiz and black turbans. Four with rifles, two with what look like swords. They have our two on their knees."*

Smith's voice came over the radio as he ran for the wall, *"Flash, 6. If they make a move, take them out. If they don't move, give us one more minute to get there."*

"6, 5. We are in place to enter."

"Roger. On our way."

Sue followed Smith as he ran to a hole in the wall that was becoming less and less distinct as the sunset turned into twilight. They were about five meters from the entrance when Sue stumbled as her prosthetic caught a rock. She fell to one knee and then freed the leg and caught up to Smith. He was already against the wall and saw her arrive. Unfortunately, when she stumbled, Sue had made a distinctive sound as her MP5 hit the rocks. Metal on stone was not a normal sound at the monastery.

Flash's voice came over the net, *"6, you need to know there are two bravos headed your way."*

Smith nodded to Sue and held up his left hand with four fingers up. Then three, then two, then one. As he closed his fist, he keyed his microphone and said, *"Go, Go, Go,"* as he and Sue pushed through the opening. Smith and Sue appeared just as the two men in black arrived at the opening. Smith fired three rounds from his suppressed .45. Two in the chest and one in the head as the black turban dropped to the ground. Sue had her suppressed MP5 selector switch set for automatic fire and four rounds stitched up the front of the second man with the last round hitting him in the chin. He was dead before he hit the ground. Sue heard rounds from the other side of the compound as Jim, Jamie and Pigpen "kinetically resolved" the other armed fighters and one of the sword wielders.

The second swordsman must have realized what was happening and decided to take at least one of the Europeans with him as he died. He had raised his blade and prepared to slash at the neck of Beroslav when he crumpled to the ground with a single bullet hole in his forehead.

"One down." Flash said to no one in particular.

Massoni and Sue were the first to reach the two men tied back to back. Massoni pulled out his Spyderco clip knife and cut the ropes, releasing the two men. He pulled the gags from their mouths and looked at them both. "We would like to leave this place fairly soon. Is that ok by you?"

"Massoni, you are such a joker," was all Jameson had to say as he got up and started to move to the opening where Jamie and Pigpen were standing guard.

Sue looked at Beroslav, "You are a hard man to kill."

"So it would appear. I hope you don't intend to make it any easier."

Sue looked straight into Beroslav's eyes and said, "I haven't decided yet."

Flash's voice came through all of their ear buds, *"In case you were wondering, this place will be crawling with bad guys soon. No turbans this time, just men in black military gear. They are at the outside wall right now opposite the way we came in. I'm thinking it is time to GTFO."*

"Roger and thanks Flash. Pull out of your location now and meet us at the trucks. Wally, you heard?"

"Roger, 6. I heard. I'm sending a couple of Tomahawks up slope to help. They will be looking for Jamie."

Smith turned to Massoni, Sue and Beroslav, "It's definitely time to go." He looked over to Beroslav who a little unsteady on his feet after some time on his knees. "Beroslav, can you run?"

"Like my life depended on it, which I suspect it does." He turned and sprinted to the opening. He was nearly there when he fell face down in the dirt. In the gloom, Sue thought he had tripped over some rocks until she heard a rifle bullet delivering the distinctive buzzing sound of "incoming." She shouted the same to everyone and then raced to Beroslav. Jameson came out from cover and helped Sue pull Beroslav behind the wall of the monastery. Massoni already had his ruck open and the field med kit in hand when they arrived. Bullets continued to impact the dirt around the wall and on the ground in front of the opening. Jameson and Sue turned Beroslav on his back and Massoni turned on a red filter flashlight to see Beroslav's injuries. He knew at once that no one could have survived the rifle round that tore an exit wound the size of a baseball from the front of Beroslav's chest. Jameson and Sue stood behind Massoni and looked at Beroslav's remains.

Jameson was the first to speak. "We talked about the threat from his competitors in Russia. I don't know if these guys are official or simply mafia, but either way, they are going to come down here to confirm the kill. We need to get out of here soonest, but Beroslav said that he had an insurance policy on board using "old school" methods. I'm thinking we need to check his boots and the seams of his jacket. After that, we need to run for it because the attackers won't want to leave any witnesses."

Pigpen and Smith pulled security at the hole in the wall, periodically returning fire when they could identify a muzzle flash at the end of the compound. If nothing else, it would prevent anyone from closing in on them. Jamie took the forward security position, green eyes on, scanning their escape route for hostiles. Massoni already had his nitrile gloves on so he checked the seams of Beroslav's clothing while Jameson checked Beroslav's boots both inside and out for a concealment. They found nothing. As they were turning away, Sue stood over the body and said, "His prosthetic. Check his prosthetic."

Massoni used his clip knife again to slice open the left sleeve. In the red light, the open sleeve revealed a sophisticated prosthetic with a number of electrodes extending into the forearm. Massoni checked the edge of the prosthetic where it mated with the arm. Nothing. He checked the prosthetic from top to bottom. Nothing. Suddenly he noticed a metallic reflection in the red light. On the prosthetic wrist was Beroslav's VDV watch. Massoni unfastened the watch and examined it. On the back were a series of engraved Russian Orthodox crosses. Massoni turned the watch on its edge which revealed what looked like a lightning connector into some internal electronics.

"Hiding in plain sight. The old school." He pocketed the watch and turned to Smith, Jameson and Sue. "I think we got it, but either way, we gotta leave."

Jamie started down slope as soon as he saw the others stand up. Sue and Jameson took one last look at Beroslav, turned and started to run down the hill. Pigpen and Smith pulled from their position and followed. Massoni was the last to leave Beroslav after he used his thumb to mark a cross on the dead man's forehead. In the dark, it was growing progressively difficult to see the trail or each other. The shadows from the exterior monastery walls made the trail appear and disappear as they ran. As they worked their way down slope in groups of three, Sue eventually changed places with Massoni and was the last one in the file. She needed to move more carefully than everyone else since every step with her left leg meant her prosthetic was receiving torque in ways that it was really not designed to handle. Sue didn't want to lose her balance again as they raced down.

Once they were clear of the exterior wall and in a dark shadow of the hillside, Jamie stopped and pulled out of a cargo pocket seven red chemical lights less than an inch long. Each one had a bit of duct tape on them. "Right shoulder please. With these IR chems on, the bird will know the good guys from the bad guys. We may need that before this is over." He noticed Beroslav was not in the mix and asked, "He stay behind?"

"Permanently," was all Massoni said as he attached the chem light to his right shoulder.

They stayed in a Ranger file and returned to the trucks along the same trail. Half way down slope, they were met by three Tomahawks who passed by them and took up defensive positions behind the team, periodically leap frogging down slope like the mountain people that they were. As they approached the trucks, Wally and Pluto were behind the wheels and had the engines running. The team slid into the back of the trucks. Smith did a head count of the SOF team and Jamie did the same for his Tomahawks. They turned to each other, gave a thumbs up and jumped into their respective shotgun positions in the two trucks. The cargo trucks rolled down the tractor trails and onto the village road and headed west toward the border.

CHECKMATE

I f the truck ride toward Takht Bhai was unpleasant, the return trip was even more so. What had been a hot and dusty daylight drive was now a hot and dusty night race to Afghanistan with the possibility that they were being pursued by an assassination team from an unknown adversary with unknown capability. Added to that, they expected sooner rather than later the Pakistani authorities as well as most of the extremist tribals in the areas would begin hunting two trucks full of invaders. Finally, as the adrenaline wore off, came the knowledge that only one of the two individuals they had tried to save was going to make it home to safety.

Just before they reached the end of the paved roads and headed into the mountainous areas, Jamie stopped the lead truck and walked to the back of the rear truck. His head and shoulders appeared over the gate. "Hey, there is a cardboard box inside there up against the cab. Slide it back here, please." Sue and Flash grabbed the box and pushed its heavy contents toward Jamie who reached into the box with both hands and pulled out two dozen black objects that looked like jacks from a children's game.

"Road nails. High quality stuff from our Klingon bag of tricks though you can make them at home if you want. These are painted with non-reflective paint so that they are hard to see at night even with the best of headlights. Excuse me while I distribute them."

Jamie disappeared from view and then reappeared farther to their rear, distributing the nails the way a farmer might sow seeds. Once completed, he ran past the truck, waving at Sue and Flash, and returned to his position in the lead vehicle. They drove off knowing that any pursuer would be delayed by at least one if not many flat tires.

As they climbed the trail, Sue and Flash watched as three sets of headlights headed in their direction. The headlights belonged to either SUVs or pickup trucks. And, they were definitely gaining on their two trucks. When the pursuing headlights reached the end of the paved road, all three sets of headlights spun off and stopped.

"Road nails. Good idea that I'm taking home with me," was all Flash said.

Rather than heading to the safehouse in Asadabad, Jamie recommended they return to FOB Pech. It was more easily defended, it was registered as a friendly compound on both OGA and USMIL records and it had a working landing zone. The Asadabad safehouse had none of these features. Smith agreed and after a brief stop on the Afghan border to change drivers and let all passengers stretch their legs, they rolled along a new dirt track to the FOB. They arrived just as the sun was rising. The security force of Tomahawks greeted their fellow militiamen as if they had been gone for years and the adventure stories appeared to begin well before tea was made. The Americans headed to the TOC and the housing area as the SF team members helped them unload their equipment. Smith decided that there was no good reason to push his team given they hadn't had any sleep for nearly two days. "Get your head down now," he said. "1500hrs, coffee, food and debrief. Check?"

Everyone nodded as they headed to their rooms. Massoni grabbed Jameson as he followed them and said, "The boss wants a brief chat, Bill. I hope you don't mind."

"I expected as much Jim. I will follow you."

They met in the TOC where Smith and Jamie were waiting. Like Smith, Jamie had sent Wally to bed. There would be plenty of work tonight and tomorrow and at least one of them needed some sleep.

"Chief, I realize you need a bath, some food and some sleep, but there are a couple of things I need to sort out before I send a note to Bagram. Honestly, I'm surprised I haven't heard from C/SOF yet since I suspect he was monitoring the net throughout. Can you hold up for a little while longer while I put an initial report together?"

"Sure, sir. We definitely do not want to piss off higher at this point."

"Excellent. So, I reckon the best way to do this is to run it from start to finish for about twenty minutes and then let me ask some questions."

Jameson started from the beginning of his kidnapping and ran the story from Tor Kham, through the Mohmand Agency, Asadabad and eventually to Takht Bhai. When he got to Takht Bhai, he described the events leading up to the rescue and said, "I figured we were goners. Especially when I saw the two Taliban seniors sharpening Khyber knives and setting up a video."

"Did Beroslav say anything else? Anything at all about these guys or about the guys that eventually killed him?"

"He apologized for being so stupid and assuming Takht Bhai would not be a Pakistani Taliban stronghold. He said his smuggling sources had told him that it was still held by Swat Sufis. He also said that he had expected to die, but from a Russian bullet instead of a Khyber knife."

"Well, he was right about that in the end," Massoni said.

"So, how did the Russians know to follow him to Takht Bhai? I get the Taliban and even the ambush on the highway which could have been other smugglers looking to take advantage of a remote place. I still don't get how the Russians figured out we were there."

Smith said, "Bill, I don't know any way that it could have happened unless our communications were compromised or someone in Beroslav's crew was on the Russian payroll. We could have another fink in our network, though I hate to think that. Also, we still don't know if this was Russian official action or just another Russian mafia adversary."

"If Beroslav was right, it was a Russian official effort. He said he intended to trade a boatload of information in exchange for the USG accepting him as a defector. He knew he had to bring out some real gems if we were going to accept him after what he did to Sue and to our assets in Cyprus."

"We will have to wait until this evening to check that out. I want my tech gurus to be fresh when they open the files just in case Beroslav put traps in the device. We have locked it up and we will do the needful starting at 1800hrs. That will do for now, Bill. Get your head down and we will get you outta here tomorrow assuming we can get a helicopter from Bagram. After that, be prepared because you are going to go through more debriefings there."

"Check, boss. I realize there are plenty of questions to be answered." Jameson walked out of the TOC and headed toward the sleeping area. Massoni followed him. They met Sue at the stairwell. She gave Jameson a bear hug and started to cry. Massoni caught Jameson's eye and they both looked embarrassed.

Back in the TOC, Smith opened his laptop, dialed in a number on the SATCOM rig and waited until the screen confirmed that he had a link to SOF/Bagram. For now, all he had was good news for the Command and that meant that he could keep it short and sweet. After that, he would have to write one more message and that one wouldn't be as pleasant or as well received. No one wanted to hear that there might be another penetration of SOF or OGA. It wasn't something he had expected so he would spend some time thinking through what he would say.

T he team was up well before 1500hrs and sharing their perspectives on the adventures of the past days. Sue was the most relieved but also the most torn by the events. On the one hand, Jameson was alive, well and safe. On the other, Beroslav, her most hated enemy, literally died in her arms as he tried to defect. The twists and turns of this plot were more than she could fathom. Not for the first time, Sue hoped that this episode would finally allow her to move back to the "normal" world of finding, fixing and finishing terrorists. She expressed these thoughts earlier that morning to Flash as they dressed in their shared room.

"What?" Flash said. "A normal life for an O'Connell? I think not, girl. But, you can certainly hope for the best. Right now, I am more than willing to bet you are one turn away from some other misadventure."

"Thanks for the expression of confidence."

"Don't mention it. You haven't spent enough time with me after I get out of bed to know what I'm like before coffee. Now, let's get downstairs before the first pot is finished and we have to wait for the second."

At 1600hrs, Smith walked into the room, grabbed a coffee cup, filled it and sat down. The team assembled at that point with the addition of Jamie, Wally and Jameson. Smith started the meeting in his standard 171 commander Jedidiah Smith style. No introductions, no polite interlude, just work.

"Here's what we need to do RFN. I want Pluto and Flash to go after what we believe is Beroslav's material that he loaded into the memory drive in his watch. I don't want anyone to bother them as they work through this and start printing material. I suspect Beroslav put some traps and even some heavy encryption into the mix on his files. Jamie, if we need help from OGA headquarters, can we get it?"

"Sure, Colonel. Of course, right now it's morning in Washington, but I suspect Flash and Pluto will have to work late. But don't worry, I have no problem bringing headquarters guys back into work."

"If we can get Melissa Nez, I would love that, sweetie." Flash smiled her most polite smile.

Smith looked at Jamie and then at Flash. "Jamie, possible?"

"Beats me, Colonel. But I will try."

"Try hard," was all Flash could say.

Smith turned to the rest of the room. "I need to assemble your thoughts on this operation from start to finish. The good, the bad, the ugly, the curious, and the dangerous. This was a successful but dangerous operation that we need to explain to the Commander in Balad, the DC in Bagram, and heaven only knows who inside the IC in Washington. I suspect by now there is already a pissed off COS in Islamabad pounding the table on why we did what we did. I want each of you to write down your own observations. I need them sent to me by 2000hrs tonight so I can put my own thoughts and summary on top and send them to higher. The important point from my perspective is we were in "hot pursuit" of Mr. Jameson and barely made it in time to save his life. I think we can all agree that working through multiple agencies and two different embassies and two liaison services that don't get along would not have delivered a positive result."

Jameson added, "Positive result means I would not be here today in case you missed that point."

"Exactly. So, please do not speculate on what coordination took place or didn't take place. That is my job to explain. Check?" Everyone nodded. Basically, Smith intended to take the hit for an unsanctioned cross-border operation. "So, get to your laptops and start writing. Jim, come with me." Smith walked out of the TOC with Massoni following. Once they were outside the TOC, Smith said to Massoni, "Jim, we need to get Jameson out of here pronto. Please work with Jamie to do the needful about getting a bird from here to Bagram direct. I don't want a stop anywhere and I don't care if it is an OGA bird or one of ours. Got that one?"

"Sure, boss. I started on that before you got up."

"Now, the real question is how did the Russians or whoever they used as their surrogates get to Takht Bhai just after us? For that matter, given what Jameson said about the actions in Cyprus last year and his capture in Tor Kham, it looks like these guys have been on us for months. I don't think we have a fink in our immediate team, but I do think there is no explanation other than some sort of leak or a piece of technology working against us. Thoughts?"

"Boss, I only have a couple of thoughts. First, the Cyprus stuff could have been remnants of that double agent that Sue and her crew uncovered months ago. For that reason, I think we focus only on our actions here in theatre. Second, since the UAVs were tracking both Bill's GPS tag and our travel, if the satellite feed from the UAV was captured, the Russians would have been, more or less, traveling along the same route we were. Of course, if they had Bill's GPS tag all along, that might explain their work last year in Cyprus. Third, I can think of an explanation for the recent chase coming from Beroslav himself. You know it is possible they tagged Beroslav somewhere along the way and followed their own tag to Takht Bhai. If Beroslav was already a hunted man, he brought them on site because of a mistake he made or some political or military wrangling in Moscow. If that is the case, we are never going to sort this out. Finally, there is always the chance that there is a Russian penetration of the Klingons or of SOF, but one thing is certain, the idea of a fink in our midst here doesn't tally. Nobody, not our team, not the OGA guys, not even the Tomahawks had an opportunity along the way to relay how it was unfolding. No chance.

"Jim, that's why I keep you around. You may be a geezer, but you distill the chaos down to simple solutions. Thanks."

"Boss, I think that was a compliment, but I'm not sure."

"Take it and run, Jim." Massoni went back into the TOC and Smith went outside to watch the sunset in the Konar.

By 0500hrs, they had confirmation that Commander, SOF had received the reports on Jameson's rescue. He responded to the message by sending his congratulations and his confirmation that he would handle any "bureaucratic" issues, as he put it, in his channels. At 0545hrs, a pair of SOF Blackhawks traveling with a pair of Apache gunships picked up Jameson and took him back to Bagram for debriefing, medical checkups and then on to CONUS for further meetings. Pigpen flew with him as his escort but mostly to get him on a plane and headed toward Europe as soon as possible. Smith wanted him back in HOA as soon as possible. There were plenty of 171 missions supporting SOF operations in the region and Pigpen was their guy.

Smith told the team it looked like nothing but good news so far. Smith walked over to the work stations where Pluto and Flash were working on Beroslav's watch. "Flash, did you hear what I said? Nothing but good news, SO FAR. Any chance you can give me more good news sometime this decade?"

Flash was in a teleconference with Melissa Nez at Agency headquarters. She had on a full headset with a small boom microphone and she was staring at her laptop with a split screen of Melissa's face and lines of computer code. She had seen Smith's reflection on the screen, so she pulled off her headset, smiled her Cheshire cat smile and said, "Boss, did you say something?"

"I saw the note that you sent me saying *Genius at work*. I was wondering how long the genius might be working before I know what the heck you are working on. It's a small thing, but as your commanding officer, periodically, I like to know what you are doing." Smith smiled back at Flash.

Massoni was across the room sitting next to Jamie and Sue. "I see this all the time. Generally, Flash comes out the winner."

"Twenty bucks says Smith gets the win this time." Jamie was reaching into his wallet.

"It's a dope's bet, Jamie. Flash always wins," was all Sue could say.

Across the room, Smith turned and walked back toward them while shaking his head.

Massoni asked, "Good news, Boss?"

"Beats me. She threw some crypto-cyber-geek speak at me and I don't know if she was making the words up or if she was really answering the question. She's been working all night on this stuff, so I don't even know if she knows if she is making sense."

Sue looked at Jamie. He shook his head.

"How about this for a question, Boss. Were we right to take the watch?"

"Oh, that's certain, O'Connell. The watch had a small lightening connector which folded into the back. Probably would have been wicked uncomfortable for a real wrist, but since it was on Beroslav's prosthetic, it hardly mattered. Pluto and Flash used the connector to download whatever was on it onto a spare memory drive Jamie had. There were two questions that I guess haven't been answered yet. First, does the download include some sort of malicious software. If so, they don't want to do any manipulation using either our computers or the OGA computers. Second, does the download have any traps that will erase the material if the traps are not removed first. I guess Ms. Nez from OGA is working on the second question while Pluto and Flash are working on the first."

"I don't know if they know how long this is going to take," Smith added with a tone of concern. "It would be nice to see some of the material soon because I want to be sure we are not going to become the hunted in the same way Beroslav was hunted."

"Colonel, I reckon you can count on being the hunted," Jamie said. "I sent the Tomahawks out to the border this morning, basically to serve as a tripwire for us. They have already reported back that there is more activity than usual among the smugglers and extremists. So far, the news is that they haven't located us yet, but they did send a couple of teams into Beroslav's residence in Asadabad and our safe-house. Not so safe anymore, which is sad, because it took Wally half a year to find a place in the city. I suspect it will only be a matter of time before this place is identified. How long? I can't even begin to guess."

"Perfect. I have data I can't access. I don't even know if it is worth accessing. I have folks hunting us and I don't know how long we have."

Jamie smiled and said, "We aim to please." He paused to have a drink of coffee. "Look at the bright side, Colonel. We have the Tomahawks on our side and they are definitely a solid fighting force. Plus, we have the OGA armed UAVs keeping watch. It's all good."

The crump of a mortar round hitting on the hillside leading up to the compound interrupted Jamie's second drink of coffee. "Or, I could be completely wrong." The second round hit the wall of the compound. "Terrific. They are walking in the mortar fire. I suspect they won't be long before they are coming into the compound. Time for me to get on the radio."

As Jamie walked away, Sue yelled across the room, "But who? Who is walking rounds into the compound?"

Jamie looked back at her and said, "Does it really matter? We can definitely say it is someone who doesn't like us, right?"

Flash and Pluto pulled off their headsets and faced Smith, Massoni and Sue. Flash said, "Were you yelling at me?" The first round to hit the compound exploded at that point.

"Nope, I was asking Jamie who was shooting at us."

Pluto said in his characteristic whisper, "Probably someone who doesn't like us."

Massoni interrupted before someone got hurt, "Can you continue this work in whatever safe room Jamie has on the compound?" Another round exploded in the middle of the HLZ.

"Looks like we are going to have to do so." Flash put her headset back on and started talking to Melissa Nez at the Agency headquarters. She shut down the communications link, shut down the USB port that was linking her laptop to the stand-alone drive and then pulled the cable that linked the two devices. She closed her laptop down and grabbed her computer bag from the table behind her. Shoving her laptop, the hard drive and the watch with the cable attached to the lightning port and the hard drive all into her bag, Flash stood up and said to Smith, "Where do you want us to go?"

Massoni was already at the far end of the room at the door leading to the quarters and the supply room. "This way, please. Flash and Pluto get new quarters. No view, no power, no danger. It's all good."

Smith and Sue moved in the opposite direction following Jamie down a hallway to a stand-alone communications center that he used with the Tomahawks. Jamie was on the radio to his militiamen, barking orders in Dari and listening to reports. Wally was just outside the room, assembling the Tomahawk force and half of the Special Forces detachment that was on base, preparing to defend the compound from any ground attack that would follow the mortars.

"Jamie, it's your base. How do you want us to help?"

"Colonel, if you could work with the ODA, that would be great. The ODA commander is out with the other half of his team working his village stability operations. I'm certain that the ODA can do their part, but they might appreciate some additional SOF operators. Good with you?"

"Check, Jamie. We will be working out there as soon as we get our kit." Smith and Sue went back through the TOC and into the living quarters. Sue disappeared into her room and pulled out her MP5 as well as her Glock in a drop holster. She put on her body armor that doubled as a load-bearing vest and confirmed all the magazines in the vest were loaded and ready to go. She put in her ear bud so that she could receive team communications and put on her ballistic glasses. If this was going to be a serious firefight, she didn't want to be out of the fight because of shrapnel or flying rocks. She grabbed Flash's long gun case and shouldered Flash's ruck that had the ammo, optics and Flash's body armor. Smith came out of his room with his own rifle and kit as well as Massoni's. "We'll pick up Pluto's kit on the way down. He stashed his in the TOC."

Mortar rounds were landing throughout the compound and there was sporadic gunfire coming from the defenders inside the compound. Smith turned to Sue and said, "I'm going over to the ODA location. Deliver the weapons to Flash and Massoni, go into the TOC and get Pluto's kit. Sort out who can come and who must stay to protect the data and once you figure that out, join the fun wherever you think it makes the most sense."

All Sue could think of at that moment was: "Commander's Intent." When she was in the 18th Airborne Corpsproviding intelligence support to a three star general and multiple subordinate division commands, commander's intent was complex and filled with what Sue thought was confusing "milspeak." Once she joined SOF, it was clear that commander's intent would be brief and pointed "Go. Do. Ask for help when you need it. And win."

All she had to say to Smith was, "Roger, boss" as she turned back toward the interior room where Massoni had taken Flash and Pluto.

When she got to the room, Flash and Pluto were already working on capturing and compressing as much data as possible so they could send a burst communication to Bagram as soon as possible. Sue looked at Massoni and said, "How busy are they?"

Flash responded, "Very busy, thank you."

Sue handed Massoni the long gun case along with Flash's weapons bag. "I reckon you know how to use this, no?"

"Yes, I do. Leave your MP5 for Flash. Take my M4. Pluto needs his kit as well. Let's get them settled and then see what we can do from the roof, eh?"

Sue ran to the TOC, retrieved Pluto's weapon and body armor and came back. Flash looked at Sue and said, "We really could use a SATCOM link from the roof while you are up there. Any chance you could run a cable up to the roof to make that happen?"

Sue nodded and said, "Going up there anyhow. You have the rig and the cable?"

Flash passed her a black bag with the antenna system and a reel of coaxial cable that would link the antenna to her computer. "Long enough, I think. You will hear me screech if it isn't."

"Screeching is so unladylike," was all Sue could think to say as she ran up the stairs to the hatch leading to the roof. Massoni was already up on the roof with the Remington and was already in action.

"Set up their antenna and then get over here and give me some target data to use with this gun."

"Check, Jim."

SATCOM rigs are relatively easy to use: Pull out the antenna, point it in the general direction of the satellite and then adjust the antenna to get the correct signal strength. It always reminded Sue of her visits to her grandfather who refused to sign up for cable tv and used a rooftop antenna to get the local news. Adjust it until the "snow" went away and the picture cleared. Sue did the needful and when she didn't hear a screech from Flash, she ran over to Massoni's fighting position.

"What do we have Jim?"

"If I can get a bit of ranging, I can work on the mortar crew that is doing "hip shoot" firing." While mortar gunnery can be as scientific as artillery, "hip shoot" or "direct lay" firing basically is a point, shoot, experiment process against a close-in target. Massoni continued, "In this case, the mortar crew is under a thousand yards. Not an easy shot, but something that can be done with a Remington. So, Sue, DO YOU HAVE A RANGE YET?"

Sue pulled out the laser rangefinder from Flash's bag of tricks. She placed the laser designator on one of the gunners working to the left of the mortar tube. "Target to the left of the tube is at 850 yards. Doesn't look to be any cross wind, but you have to shoot about 20 degrees down slope."

"Calculated the downslope part of the equation while you were diddling with the SAT rig. OK, 850 yards." Sue watched through the scope as she saw in her peripheral vision the recoil from the Remington on Massoni's shoulder and heard the slight cough from the suppressed rifle. The gunner dropped holding his thigh.

"You hit him in the femur. He's out of the game. Second target to the right of the tube. 848 yards."

"Roger, 848 yards. Up one click to adjust for the previous shot." Massoni pulled the trigger and Sue saw the round impact center mass on the gunner.

"Second gunner down. Now for the ammo bearer who has figured out what is happening and starting to run away. Directly behind the tube, 862 yards."

"Roger, 862 yards and on the move. We are starting to push my limits. Let's see." The Remington went off and Sue saw the gunner fall to the ground holding his right leg.

"Looks like you hit him in the shin. He's down for a while." Sue heard Massoni work the action on the Remington and a second shot followed. This round hit the man on the ground in the shoulder.

"Good enough," was all Massoni would say. "Now we need to scan for the guys who are using the mortar attack as the diversion to get closer. Any sign?"

Sue looked out at the hillside. She didn't see anyone except the Tomahawks swarming out of the compound and down the hill. "Nothing out there but the Tomahawks."

The noise from the helicopter came suddenly. Sue was used to this sort of transition from the SOF "Little Birds," five bladed MH6 helicopters that could carry a four man raid team. The muffler system on the turbines was designed to ensure there was no warning until the aircraft was overhead. She had never seen a similar system on a Russian helicopter as big as an Mil7, but the black bird that was headed her way was quiet. Very quiet.

"Jim, raiders to our front."

"Got it." He sent a round into the cockpit just as the helicopter flared overhead and began to stabilize for the fast rope to come out of the back of the bird and start to deliver raiders. The first man was on the rope when the helicopter started to rotate counterclockwise in a barely controlled spin. Massoni sent another round into the cockpit as it became visible again.

After the second round, the helicopter lost stability and began to sway back and forth as well as rotate in circles. Men who had been on the tailgate of the helicopter started falling out of the bird, grabbing for the fast rope and usually missing. Men in black jumpsuits landed in the compound; some completely immobile, some with broken limbs.

Sue could see that one of the pilots was fighting to keep his bird stable. Rather than crash into the compound, he chose to veer off toward the hillside in hope of landing in more open terrain. He didn't succeed. The bird landed on its side and the turbines began the process of beating the rotors into the soil, sending shards of metal from the main rotor, the tail rotor and eventually the engine turbine blades in all directions. Fire was the last step in the tragedy. Meanwhile, the Tomahawks and the six members of the ODA were engaging those raiders who were capable of fighting back. Massoni kept his scope on the horizon.

"If there is one bird, there is a second bird. You know the helicopter rule — two is one and one is none."

"That's only if this is a military operation."

"And if it isn't a military operation, it is a pretty good copy of one."

Sue used the rangefinder to scan the horizon. She finally found the second bird. "Hovering about 5000 yards away. It looks like they are observing and don't want to engage."

"Don't count on it, Sue. There is always the possibility that they intend to use a Sagger."

Sue watched as a small flash occurred on the left side of the helicopter. She could see a missile headed their way. "Jim, they fired one at us. I don't have a clue where it's going."

"You won't until it hits. It's a wire guided missile with the gunsight in the cockpit of that bird. Let's hope it isn't aimed at us." As Sue watched, the missile closed in on the compound and then dove into the ground about 200 yards short of the compound.

Massoni said, "Wire broke and they lost command of the missile. Let's see if they try again or if they just want to quit." Before they could determine what the helicopter pilots would choose, it exploded.

"Fast movers, maybe? If Jamie called in air support, this would have been an easy shot for a fast mover."

Jamie's head came up through the hatch, "Or, it might have been the first air to air success for an armed UAV. I think we are done with this drama for now. All good up here?"

Massoni said, "OGA or SOF bird?"

"I'm not telling." Jamie's head disappeared down the hatch.

"Sue, let's stay up here a bit in case we need to provide a little more support to our guys on the ground."

Sue let out a long breath that she had been holding for the last few seconds. "Whatever you say, Sergeant Major."

The briefing for the SOF commander was in the TOC at Bagram. He was currently in Balad in Iraq, so the 171 team, Jamie and Wally were asked to fly to Bagram for a SVTC. Smith was sitting to the right of the SOF deputy commander as they faced the three large plasma screens labeled BRAGG, BALAD, and OGA. Seated to the left of Smith were Massoni, Pluto, Flash and Sue. To the left of the deputy commander were his staff, the COS in Kabul, his chief of operations, Jamie and Wally. Sue had gotten used to the prompt nature of SOF SVTCs and this was no different. As the digital clock on the tent wall displayed 1200Z, all three screens came on. The Bragg screen focused on the SOF chief of staff who was working in the SOF Main TOC fondly known as "the tank." The Balad screen was focused on the SOF Commander. The OGA screen had three individuals, the only one Sue recognized was Melissa Nez.

"Sir, we are here to give you a quick AAR on the operations out of FOB Pech the past few days."

"Thanks. Hello Jed. It's good to see you. I understand you have quite an intel coup but it didn't come easily."

Smith looked at the deputy commander who nodded to him. "Sir, while we were not able to save the Russian defector Nicolai Beroslav from his attackers, he did provide a gigabyte of data on Russian organized crime efforts providing material and financial support to Iran's Islamic Revolutionary Guards Corps, Hizballah, and the Taliban. The crime syndicate has direct links to senior Russian leadership. The Russians tried to stop our collection in Cyprus by attacking our team there. They were not successful, but their actions triggered

Beroslav's decision to defect. Now, we have names, dates, locations, as well as mobile and landline phone numbers, tail numbers of aircraft and ship names. It will be an excellent start in an effort to dismantle this network."

"I understand it took a serious amount of brain power from your team as well as from Langley. Once again, it was Flash and Ms. Nez in this work, am I correct?"

"Yes sir, along with another of my analyst, SFC Jackson."

"Well done, all. I am always pleased to see this sort of teamwork between the Command and our Agency colleagues. In your initial report, you said that you were working out of an Agency base in the Konar."

The deputy commander commented, "It's a joint Agency and Special Forces base, sir."

"More partnerships, more successes." On the screen it was clear that the commander was using the joystick at his desk to move the camera round. It settled on Sue.

"Chief O'Connell. It seems anytime we have an odd, but successful operation, you are in the middle of it. Is that right?" The commander smiled.

Smith gave Sue a look that implied "SAY SOMETHING!"

Sue swallowed and said, "It would appear I am a bit of a magnet for odd ops, sir."

The SOF commander laughed out loud and the camera swung back to his deputy and to Smith. *"Jed, I think you are lucky to have a SOF odd op intel magnet in your shop. Keep her busy, please."*

"Yes, sir. I intend to do so," was all Smith had to say.

After the briefing, the team met for a few minutes to say goodbye with the standard "See you on the other side." Everyone knew that there would be little if any break before they started on another high intensity project, so no one was interested in heading to any of the fast food joints on Bagram Airbase. It would be a meal in the dining facility and then some down time in one of the temporary duty barracks on post followed by a return flight. Jamie and Wally took off back to FOB PECH as soon as they had dinner.

The commander's G5 was off on another critical mission, so they would be going back to Ramstein Airbase in Germany via sling seats on a C17. As the team confirmed departure time Massoni decided to have a little fun with this tired bunch, "Hey, once we get to Ramstein, we can probably grab a C130. Anyone interested in a hollywood jump into Italy? The airborne brigade there has drop zones and it will cover us on jump pay for another 90 days!" It was not clear who threw the first styrofoam cup a the sergeant major, but in the end, he had to dodge cups from Smith, Pluto, Flash and Sue.

Sue picked up her helmet bag that she had left behind in a SOF locker in Bagram. The bag doubled as her field brief case. She started to trudge over to the barracks. She was well and truly exhausted.

As she walked away from the SOF command post, she heard a pinging noise from inside the bag. She looked into the bag and saw her Cyprus-based mobile phone. Sue usually carried her phone in a waterproof bag and left it at the last secure location before going downrange. In this case, it had been in Bagram. On her return, she sent a text to her mother saying all was well. Over the years, Barb O'Connell had told Sue, "I don't want or need to know when or where you are heading downrange. I just want to know when you are done and safe." So, Sue complied as often as she could. Bagram Airbase had a mobile hotspot for the troopers in transit and she had decided it was safe enough to give her Mom an "I'm safe and headed home" message. It appeared her mom had responded. Sue looked down at the text message.

The text message said: *Sue, Glad you are safe. We need to talk. New family business. Mom*

Sue's heart sank. Family business for the O'Connells never meant good news.

J.R. SEEGER is a western New York native who served as a U.S. Army paratrooper and as a CIA case officer for a total of 27 years of federal service. In October 2001, Mr. Seeger led a CIA paramilitary team into Afghanistan. He splits his time between western New York and Central New Mexico.